Baby Mother and the King of Swords

Baby Mother and the King of Swords

Lorna Goodison

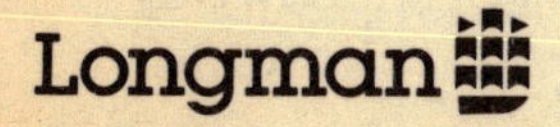

Longman Group (UK) Limited,
Longman House, Burnt Mill, Harlow,
Essex CM20 2JE, England

Longman Jamaica Ltd,
95 Newport Boulevard,
Newport West, PO Box 489,
Kingston 10, Jamaica

Longman Caribbean (Trinidad) Ltd,
Boundary Road, San Juan, Trinidad
and Associated Companies throughout the world

First published 1990

ISBN 0 582 05492 3
Produced by Longman Group (FE) Limited
Printed in Hong Kong

British Library Cataloguing in Publication Data
Goodison, Lorna
Baby mother and the king of swords.
I. Title
813 [F]
ISBN 0-582-05492-3

Library of Congress Cataloging-in-Publication Data
Goodison, Lorna.
Baby mother and the king of swords/Lorna Goodison.
p. cm.
ISBN 0-582-05492-3
1. Jamaica—Fiction. I. Title.
PR9265.9.G6B34 1990
813—dc20 89-12199
CIP

Contents

The King of Swords 1

The Dolly Funeral 7

I come through 12

Pinky's fall 18

Follow your mind 21

I don't want to go home in the dark 29

A wise man 33

The Big Shot 37

Moon 46

By love possessed 50

From the clearing of possibility 57

Angelita and Golden Days 62

Shilling 69

Bella makes life 75

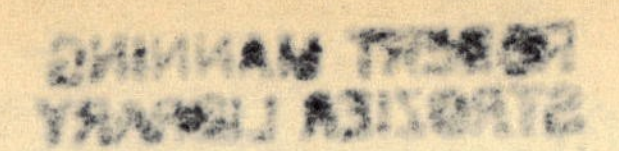

Dedication
To all the Baby Mothers who insisted that I tell their stories. And for the gracious spirit who leads us into understanding.

Acknowledgements
To the University of Iowa International Writing Programme 1983, for the fellowship which enabled me to write some of these stories, and to Bill and Trish Hewitt; also to the Bunting Institute, Radcliffe College where I completed these stories – thanks.

The King of Swords

How skilled that man is with a sword. How expertly he inflicts a wound of a word at a time when you are most vulnerable and unsuspecting. Like one night you are all dressed to go out and because the budget is tight and you have not had anything new for a while, you have done your best with everything but your shoes, which are looking a little tired. And his eyes sweep you up and down and he says nothing about your hair (which everyone admires) or your slim figure (from overwork) but comes down on your shoes and mutters, '. . . those shoes . . . .' so you spend the rest of the night hiding your feet; so he asks you loudly, 'What's wrong with your feet ?'

I finally figured out who he reminds me of: 'Aunt B'. He'd die if he heard that. He fancies himself as a very masculine man. But he does remind me of Aunt. They both have eyes which are cold and sharp like a hen's, and they both seem unable to live peacefully with other people . . . unable to live peacefully inside themselves so they must always be hacking at everyone around them. It's as if they are terrified of what they will find if they sit quietly with themselves . . . so they live on others.

I am ten years old. I am filled with life. I like to jump up and down on the same spot and skip rope till my calves hurt or just run for ever like horses do.

I should have been a country child . . . you can't run very far in the city . . . still I like to run . . . around and around the playfield at school, to the shop to buy bread and back . . . I'm always going somewhere very fast. People say, 'This little girl fiery eh?' and Aunt says, 'She is wicked and bad, it's because you don't know her.' There is something which Aunt sees in me as very,

very bad and wicked . . . this thing is contained in my appearance. It's in my eyes which they say are bright . . . and my smile which appears quickly and my body (I'm small and thin for my age), but sometimes I feel like electric currents are moving in waves through my body . . . sometimes I feel like I could fly . . . and sometimes I dream I am floating in the air . . . above the streets . . . above the gully with the dead dogs and the unemployed men sitting on the bridge and the people selling fruits and cigarettes and sweeties . . . above Lola and Violet who sell their bodies on Thursday which is Ben Johnson day and things are really tight . . . no food in the house then. And I have 'the eye' . . . I'm always seing things that nobody else sees. I once heard Aunt (she is not really my aunt, I just call her that). I once heard her telling one of her friends about me and the brother of one of my friends. He was at least twenty, I was ten almost eleven . . . she said, 'He looks at her the way a big man looks at a big woman, and she so bold, she just look right back into him face.' That was not true, I never could look him in the face because I was terrified of what I saw there.

She saw me looking at her when she spoke, and she shot me a glance of such venom that I immediately crossed my arms over my chest. It was as if I had to protect my heart and the small swellings which were growing on my chest. When she looked at me like that, I always felt wicked and dirty. I already knew I was not as clean as my brother . . . she had screamed at me one day not to use the same towel as him; she also washed the men's and the women's clothes separately.

I lived with Aunt . . . because my parents were in England. One day soon they were going to send for me. Occasionally they would send me parcels with pretty clothes. When I dressed up in them, I seemed to incur her wrath even more. She would say things about 'rendering your heart and not your garments' as I went off to church. It seems to me now, that I hardly ever left her presence without carrying away words of disapproval . . . I was always trying to do something to please her, like make her cups of tea when she had gas pains; she would take the tea and then say, 'It's a pity you are so rude.' I took these remarks into me, right into my ten-year-old heart and I knew from then that I was undeserving of love, that the real me was very wicked and very bad. It occurred to me much later that maybe this woman was practising a strange kind of reverse psychology on me.

She had been very beautiful in her time. She must have been attractive to many men. Maybe she was hoping that if she told me I was bad enough times, I would want to be 'good'. It was the same thing that made people say that a baby was 'ugly' when it was really pretty, because that way you would fool the bad spirits which want to follow beauty, also, to say that a thing was pretty was somehow boasting, and the proud get cut down. But, you see, I had this great need for things to be true. I took her words for their obvious meaning.

I never ever back-answered this woman, not ever. I had worked it out that one day soon my parents were going to send for me to go to England and join them. I was going to go on the boat my mother went on. You see, my father had gone first and then he had written to say that my mother should come. She didn't want to leave us, but the money was not enough for me, my brother and her. So she would go and work some money and send for us. The day she was leaving, I tried to be brave. I went on the boat with her, it was called the *Sea Change* . . . it looked so shiny and clean and pretty. I wanted with my whole heart to be going with my mother on this shining ship to the faraway land where people claimed it was so cold you had to wear as many as five sweaters at a time and when you spoke, steam came out of your mouth. Then my mother just hold me and my brother really tight and asked God to protect us till we could all be together again.

I didn't cry because my brother was crying so much I had to hold him. She told me to have manners to this woman, as she knew I was fiery and I took her charge seriously. So I never answer her back, not one time until that time.

I was always thinking of ways to please this woman, whom I called Aunt to make her like me. And this day, Sunday, I decided to wash up the dishes after dinner, although she didn't ask me. We had visitors after church, so she used her good plates, actually they were plates my mother had sent for us. I was washing them up by the cistern . . . when I started to think about my mother and father . . . and as I soaped the plate it was like I could see my mother's face in the plate. My mother's face is very kind . . . she smiles a lot, she is very gentle. She calls me 'little one'. . . she laughs at my antics . . . when people say I'm 'maddy, maddy', my mother says, 'Leave her, I was just like that.' She must have grown very differently though, because now she wasn't 'maddy, maddy'. She was so calm and peaceful . . . most times. I begun to cry and my mother's face dissolved into tears too and slipped away from me and out of my hands and the plate crashed into the cistern. Aunt screamed at me from upstairs. She said that my mind was divided. That is why I could not concentrate.

She said I thought I was a big woman and who had told me to wash her dishes anyway. And that day I answered her. I told her that she had a nasty mind, that she was always telling me what was really in her mind and that it was my mother who had sent the plates anyway. She ran downstairs . . . and screamed at me that I was dead to trespasses and sins. And I screamed, 'So are you, you old hige. It's like you want to suck my blood, you don't make me prosper. You are an old hige, you need my blood so that you can live.' I've identified her! All the people in the yard heard. From that day on, she hardly said one word, good or bad to me . . . she also wrote my mother and told her to take me out of her house. That was a blessing, my mother found the money and sent for me and my brother soon after. Aunt's decline was very rapid . . . it seems that she took sick a few days after we left for England and for the rest of her long life, something was always wrong with her. Many times I thought, 'I should not have answered her.' I *was* dead to trespasses and sin.

I have a history of loving men who cannot love me. I thought anybody who showed an interest in me, loved me. I badly wanted to be good, for somebody to love me because I was good.

I have put up with much from this man, his bullying, his meanness, his insistence on violating everyone around him, his hatred of himself which he transfers to others. I accept it, I accept it all because in a way I am too ashamed to admit to the world that I have chosen badly once again; from afar he looked so good, so kind. Then one afternoon we are talking, or rather he is talking and I am listening, listening to him make great detailed plans for our lives. He has several plans, he has written them out, budgeted the days of our future together. We will spend thirteen days in this place some two years from now . . . fifteen nights in this other place and a month doing this or that . . . and I listen to him and I wonder how in the world can anybody be so sure of time, so in control of the future. I ask him this and he informs me that he has plans b. and c. in case plan a. does not work and in spite of myself I laugh . . . I laugh because I come from a way of life where people always qualify the future . . . my mother will say to her sister, I will see you tomorrow . . . God willing . . . or I will go out next week if life spare. I tell him this and he laughs, he says . . . he believes in the Power of the Will . . . his will. He has a definition of the word written and put up over his desk . . . he says his favourite poem is the one which has the line 'I am the master of my fate, I am the captain of my soul.' I tell him that I read somewhere that the man who wrote those words, lived to regret writing them as fate seemed to single him out particularly for some crippling blows and that he came to realize he had no control over his fate after all. I said I prefer the last line of Robert Frost's 'Goodbye and keep cold': '. . . Some things have to be left to God.'

He roars when I mention God's name and I can see he is very angry because I am arguing with him . . . he becomes very cruel when he is crossed and something tells me he is about to do something to show me this. He gets up and goes over to a drawer and he takes from it a letter I have written to him. In the same way I was always trying to please Aunt, I am always trying to please this man; one of the ways I thought I could do this was by writing him a letter telling him about my deepest fears, about the really personal things which I had told no one about me. I ended the letter by saying I want to show you myself as I really am inside, something I've never shown to anybody. And he takes this gift and he stands in the centre of the room and he reads it out loud, in a mocking, cruel voice, he reads back all my fears and confessions to me . . . and he ends his recital by saying, that is you . . . so how can you tell me what to do? So I answered him back. For this ultimate violation I answer him back and say . . . 'You should read what I've been writing recently, they are called "letters of victory", and I'm going to win a great victory over you and her and them.' I'm thinking about the men who couldn't love me or themselves or who loved themselves to a fault. I'm thinking about Aunt. I'm thinking about him. He is livid, he says, 'who is her, who is them?' I say I'm going to win a great victory over all of you, especially you. Just for a second I see her eyes inside his, cold and hard like a hen's and I say I know who you are, old higo trying come back to claim my life again. And you, I say to him, you are the King of Swords. I have identified him . . . their hold over me will decline.

The Dolly Funeral

I can't remember how Bev and I became friends, but I remember at first feeling displaced by her as leader of our neighbourhood group of children at large, in the summer holidays. She came from a family that was even bigger than mine and up until that time I had been the child to hold that particular distinction. I had six brothers which meant people thought twice about interfering with me. Bev had eight brothers. My parents had nine children. There were twelve children in the Lyons' household, and when her family moved into the neighbourhood, she just naturally assumed the leadership role which I had held till then. I loved visiting the Lyons' house. They lived in 'their own place', which made them rich in the eyes of everyone in the neighbourhood. Their place was a many-roomed yard which was peopled by the many Lyons' married sons and daughters and a few aunts and cousins.

The first time I visited their house, I remember wishing that I lived there. Unlike my house, where somebody was always correcting you for 'sitting down bad' or 'common behaviour', the Lyons were a marvellously free and uninhibited people.

They yelled at each other, screamed with laughter and used language that would send my mother for the brown soap to scour out somebody's mouth.

The first time I witnessed Mrs Lyons trying to discipline Vavan, 'the baby' of the family, I was truly astonished. Vavan did some really dreadful thing, Mrs Lyons screamed at him to 'beyave,' he replied 'Gweyframme'. She swung a punch at him, he stuck out his tongue at her, dropped to his belly, wriggled under the bed and from his dark hideout proceeds to tell her some things no child should tell a mother and remain alive. She yelled that she was going to tear his backside and seizing a broom proceeded to stab wildly at his hidden form. She must have seen me staring at her because she paused and advised me to go outside and play in the yard, then they resumed the duel, he with the foul mouth and she with the broomstick.

All sorts of wonderful things happened at the Lyons' house. Periodic fights would break out between the brothers: big, strong Spanish-looking men, who would fight each other fiercely until their mother appeared and sometimes doused them with a goblet of cold water.

My friend Bev had all sorts of lovely toys and games to play with, but mostly she had a wonderful talent for organizing great events. These could range from the really low-level act of getting a group of children together to go and tease Rowena – the retarded child who lived several streets away (I can truly say I could never bring myself to join in this activity), to informing on Mr Frenchie to his wife, Miss Dolly, about which bar he had spent all his money in (she always told her to mind her own business and stay out of big people's business), to organizing dolls' tea parties, weddings and pregnancies, to the Dolly Funeral.

One day, towards the end of the summer holidays when it seemed we had run out of new games to play and that Bev's reputation for inspiring leadership of our group was beginning to pall, Bev came up with the idea of the Dolly Funeral. She proceeded to kill one of her less attractive dolls, by wringing its rubber neck, and placing it in a shoe box on her bed . . . 'She dead,' said Bev in a low voice, 'we going to have to bury her.' For two days the doll lay in the 'dead house' as Bev referred to the shoe box, her life all bubbled out in clouds of pink and white foam, while we prepared for the Funeral.

We searched my mother's sewing scraps for some white satin and lace material and we sewed her a lovely shroud. Bev's brother Harry proceeded to nail up a crude coffin using what looked like boards ripped from the side of the pit latrine; all arrangements for the funeral were organized by Bev.

First there would be a procession from the front gate through the middle gate (her yard had two separate sections) and down to the graveside which was situated under a huge ackee tree. I was not so thrilled to hear about the choice of this site as large rats were known to live in the ackee tree and I was more afraid of them than most other things, but I had to go along with Bev's plans.

We all went to inspect the grave site which had been dug by Harry, Bev's brother, with one of Mrs Lyons' cooking spoons. There were to be some light refreshments as it was necessary to attract as many children as possible to this event. The refreshments consisted of pieces of bulla cake and lime-less limeade known as belly-wash.

The funeral arrangements fully occupied us for two days. Bev was going to be the parson; when the boys remarked that nobody had ever seen a woman parson, she just looked at them and said, 'Is whose dolly funeral?' and they retreated. I was going to read from the Bible because I could read better than any of the other children, or so they said anyway.

My mother was not consistent when it came to allowing me to play at other people's houses. Some days for no reason, she would say, 'Don't leave the house today, sometimes you should let people long to see you.' The day of the funeral was one of those days. I got dressed to walk over to Bev's house and as I approached my mother to ask her permission/inform her where I was going, she said 'Don't leave the house, etc . . .' I pleaded with her, I enquired of her if she did not remember me telling her all about the arrangements for the funeral, how important it was that I go because I was going to read from the Bible and could she 'just please do, I beg you, mama, make me go'. My mother started the sewing machine by slapping the rim of the handle with her palm and proceeded to pump the broad flat pedal at a fierce rate. That action, read by any fool, clearly meant, 'Don't say anymore.'

So I subsided in a corner of the verandah and wept. As with each time I felt I had been dealt an injustice by my parents, I imagined that I was not their child. That I had been the victim of a careless hospital blunder and that my real parents were out there somewhere in Kingston. Nice people, who would never deprive me of the right to attend a Dolly Funeral.

As the time of the funeral approached, Bev came over to enquire why I was not present at the site, and saw me sobbing in a corner of the verandah. I told her what my mother had said, she said, hissing her teeth, 'Chuh just teef out,' and I for the first time in my life did just that, I sneaked out of the yard without my mother's permission. But I had to do it in stages. When Bev had left, I got up from my corner (after a suitable period of time) and made my move, first, to the cistern where I drank some water I did not want, then from the cistern when Miss Minnie our helper's back was turned, to the back gate where I stood for some time looking forlornly over the zinc fences and across the gully.

After stage three came the quick, bold dash to freedom. As I took to my heels and headed for Bev's house looking in no other direction but straight ahead, was it paranoia or did I really hear Miss Minnie calling, 'Don't your mother tell you not to leave the yard?'

I arrived at a very key moment in the funeral proceedings. It was near the beginning and it was nearly the ending as Vavan chopped Hugh Lawrence Brown (for some reason everybody called this boy all of his entire name all the time) in a dispute over who was to carry the coffin. It was a tiny wound really and we persuaded Hugh Lawrence Brown not to go and tell his mother. We had to bribe him by breaking the rules and giving him a whole Bulla cake for himself. He ate it right there at the start of the funeral and Harry proceeded to make a bitter remark about 'hungry belly children who just come to nyam off people food.' Apart from these set-backs, the procession went as planned. We lowered the doll into the grave and heaped up a mound of dirt over the hole. We then stuck a cross made from two fudge-sticks wired together with an elastic band at the head of the grave and we attempted to sing 'Abide with me', but nobody knew all the words, so we sang instead 'Flow gently sweet Afton', which we had all learned at school. I read Psalm 1 rather badly and too loudly because I was afraid of the rats and of the wrath of my mother, who must have found out that I was missing by now.

Even as I read, I imagined myself beneath the ground in a simple wooden box because my mother was surely going to kill me when I went home. She didn't. My father almost did. He whom I loved so much because he was never cross with me. It was the worst beating I ever received, not that he beat me badly, but to be beaten by somebody you loved so much was so humiliating. He said he had to, because I had been 'wilfully disobedient'. He forbade me to visit Bev's house for at least two weeks, and by the end of the two weeks school had started again and Bev got herself a boyfriend and told me I was a child and she couldn't play with me anymore. But I never did hear of anybody else having a Dolly Funeral, so I'm glad I went, no matter what, so there.

I Come Through

One night out at Inn on the Ocean. When I finish singing 'I come through', the place was just quiet, quiet. When I finish singing. All you could hear was the waves slapping against the concrete wall and it was like everybody in the place stopped breathing when I sing 'I come through'.

'When I nearly reach the bottom
Satan call to me and say,
you know I want you for my woman
you know you going to be mine today.
But I hold on to the promise
that my pain is only for a time.
I say, "back wey satan not me,
no, not this time".
I rise up like new
I come over, I give thanks,
I come through.'

It take a little while before the people start to clap, and then them clap like them would never stop. Clap till them almost drown out the sound of the sea . . . and some of the women and the barmaid was crying. You think is a easy thing to be a woman and a singer in this recording business? If the big, big man star them can get rob, much less a woman who don't have nobody to protect her interest like me.

I could tell you some things! Producer who you have to pay with everything you have before you can go into the studio; disc jockey who want to play with you so your record can get a air-play.

The public who feel that everything you do is their business, if you ever hear some of the things that some total stranger come up to you and ask you because them buy one of you record one time!

I can sing. If is one thing that I can do, I can sing. I sing big. I like big singing. You know how some people sing a song like them mean with it, like them swallow part of it and keep it for themself and then them lend you the rest? Not me. When I sing, I give everything. Some time when I finish singing is like I going to dead . . . it's like I give the audience my blood. But I don't know any other way . . . sometimes I think that one day I'm going to sing a song and then die right after that.

I have no luck with man. None. Most man don't like their women to be 'stars'. They love you for it, but they hate you because of it. I have no luck with man. But I love the same way I sing, completely, with everything that happen (although I could never say that I don't regret nothing). I can't regret really how I stay . . . what I have in me is like a waterfall . . . it just pour out itself from a high place and plenty time it get beat up on the rocks below . . . but it still pouring and maybe one day if I lucky, it will have caught somewhere and settle nice and peaceful in a pool of water, full of little fish and delicate waving water-flowers and anybody who weary could come and just rest themself right there.

The first man I love is the same man who tell me I could sing and him say him would be my producer. Before I record any song though, I have a baby for him and then another one and then him start to treat me very bad. Sometimes I used to wonder if this man get a calling to come and mad me. One night him put me and the little boy out in the rain . . . is a good thing the baby was with my mother. Him put me and the little boy out in the rain and sey I must go and catch man, for him spend all him money produce record with me and the record don't sell and me was of no use to him. When I stand up outside inna the rain I never exactly curse God but I had to ask him some hard questions, 'Is what I do so?' 'What make me salt so?' I give this man everything, all some thing that I never know I have, I find them and give him and all I getting is beating and shame. If it wasn't for me son, maybe I woulda do something to myself that night . . . but when I start to listen to the devil telling me to 'done it' . . . I hear my boy say, 'Mamma liff me up' . . . and so I liff him up . . . is so I get liff too.

And like a spite, is like from I begin my life with that kind of bad treatment, is like it follow me. Everyman I meet turn out to be another one who come to mad me . . . is a wonder I never really and truly mad because believe me, I come close, close, close. The last man I was along with before my life change was a man who follow me fi months. That time I never have nobody. I say I done with man. And this man follow me up and down every time I go to sing somewhere, him was there in front row in the centre a watch me. And him write me and him send message to me by all manner of everybody who know me . . . just give him a chance no? Finally I give in to him. I get pregnant . . . somehow is like they don't make a birth control yet that agree with my system. I get pregnant and this same man who follow me and beg me just to give him a chance, him look pon me and ask me if is fi him? You know I never answer him. And I never have the baby. And a write a song about it: 'Little bird, just take flight, be one now with the night. One day when I fly past pain, you and me we'll sing together again.'

Every time I take a beating I write a song (I have a lot of song). My grandmother always say that God have our tears in a bottle . . . my bottle must be demijohn. You know what a man tell me one time? Him say, 'You must make me feel guilty because I can't live up to you. I feel really bad when I do you the smallest little thing.' But I said, 'I am a human being and I know I have my bad ways too.' I don't expect that two people living together not going to have problems . . . him say yes . . . but I can't take the responsibility of hurting you – it make me feel bad, so bad that sometime I just want you to think the worse of me and leave me because I can't live up to you.

Another one say . . . My feelings come in like a baby mole . . . him fraid to do anything to hurt it so him rather leave it alone. The baby mole, that soft tender place at the top of a little baby's head. Mothers cover it and protect it . . . who was to cover me? I try to make myself tough one time. But I never get any songs. I try to 'use' people, to talk like a bad woman but I get use more than ever and is like some people just like to hear when I gwan like a bad woman . . . is like I was giving them a big joke. I work it out that I couldn't really change myself by myself but I was really trying to find a balance.

Then one night I get a vision. I dream that I see a woman at the foot of a hill, her head was pointing down and her two legs were pointing up the hill. When I look around I see that her head was resting in a pile of stinking garbage . . . a whole heap of rotten stinking rubbish. I could smell it . . . it was like the garbage of everybody in the world that she was lying down in, it was so rotten and so plenty . . . and then around her now was a ring of mawgre dog . . . the dog dem with dem ribs look like scrubbing board and them just a hanker round her and the garbage but mostly them was hankering after her . . . is like them was waiting for her to dead, with her head inna the garbage. And is like a flash reach me . . . like I see myself. . . say it was really me lying down there, for me life was little more than a pile of stinking dirty garbage. I owe money, a mad woman was sending a gunman to me say me take away her man . . . everytime I cut a song them play it two time on the radio and stop . . . mi children was not getting proper food . . . old nyaga was washing them mouth pan me more than ever . . . my name was at the top of the agenda at every meeting in J.P.'s hairdressing parlour, where barracudas gather to wash their hair and wash their mouth on other women. Them (old nyaga) say me done with, 'She mash up you see!' and mi friend them. My granny always sey when you dream see dog it mean friend. Well my 'friend' them was some mawgre dog! And I remember something else she used to say again . . . some time when life look like it out fi tumble down pan her and mash her up, she say, 'Lord, make a way,' and I say it. In mi dream I say, 'Lord make a way,' and in the dream it was like a way open in the garbage, and I find a strength and I kick we some of it myself and a find stone and I fling it after the mawgre dog them and then scatter. And I find myself standing up and when I look to my right, I see a big clean pool of water. It look like nobody ever bathe in there yet. It look blue like if God did wear a ring that would be the colour of the stone in the ring. And I take off all my clothes and I bathe and I bathe and I bathe. I wash out my clothes and I spread them on the grass to dry and I bathe till night come and then the moon come up a big round face moon and me did feel like it was all my moon, because my face round too. And the moon bring a lot of stars and she dress up the sky with them and I get all the light that I need to walk up the hill.

See hear. When I wake, I was crying. I was crying so till I feel like I was really in a pool.

Heed your dreams you hear. I couldn't want a plainer dream than that. I get up and I bathe and dress and I beg my mother to keep me children and I take a bus to the country where my grandmother bury and I find her grave and I spend the most part of one whole day sitting down on the tomb and I tell her everything and I say I want me life to change . . . gran gran, help me with the mawgre dog and the rubbish I am in . . . help me.

And is like I hear her saying . . . stop sing for a time, take back your pearls from before the swine and come out of the world until you can go back into the world.

Seven years I live in country. I plant my granny field. I build up back her little house and me and the pickney them fit into the community. Nobody never know me down there as no singer . . . them just know me as my grandmother favourite grand-daughter. And them just accept me and help me and laugh and quarrel and cry with me and you want to know sey right before my granny house there was a hill look like the hill in mi dream, and yes there is a pool.

Them say I come late . . . 'where she was all the time?' 'Mi did think she dead.' Plenty of the young people dem never know me . . . 'you ever hear a singer name . . . (me)?' By this time my boy turn man and him also turn mi manager. What I learn in seven years . . . what I learn in the seven years I come out of the world so that I could come back for my fullness within the world . . . what I learn can hold under the cover of one word . . . LOVE. That is a subject that can take a lifetime to study and you will probably never done. For love is a light that have to catch in you first. And then I will tell you about it in my songs. That's another thing . . . when I was out of the world I get a new kind of song and a new kind of singing. If you hear me and you knew me before, maybe you might not know me now. I still sing big but now singing uplifts me. I don't want to dead when I finish. Some people say I know things. I know one thing. I come through.

Pinky's Fall

If anything, Miss Chin looked more like an Indian. She might have had some distant Chinese relatives somewhere in her blood lines, but she claimed even stronger Chinese ancestry than her husband, Mr Chin, who could speak almost no English and had not too long come from Hong Kong.

Miss Chin used to sit in the grocery shop which she operated with Mr Chin, and she would a talk a lot. At least it seemed that way to me. Every time my mother would send me to buy a tin of condensed milk or a thick, white, hard dough-bread for supper, she would be sitting in the shop talking loudly to whoever happened to be there. Invariably she was holding forth upon the same topic, the dirty nasty ways of other people's children. And as always, in the same way you said 'amen' at the end of a prayer or 'goodbye' when you were leaving a place, she would seal her dissertation with a short or long hymn on the virtues of her daughter Pinky.

Now depending on who was listening (and some poor person was always listening), she could go on for a very long time upon this subject. If the person listening was trying to credit some groceries, she made them listen for a very long time and they, naturally wanting to get the food, would agree with her, the intensity of their agreement depending on the urgency of their need for the food.

Some people though, like my mother, she never tried that with. My mother did not believe in trusting food. She had a proper shop book and she took her groceries each week and paid promptly for them at the end of the next week. Also my mother had a lot of children and since Miss Chin's problem centred around the dreadful, disgusting, awful behaviour of other people's children, she tended to leave our family alone . . . besides, we were not ordinary as my mother never ceased to tell us and, somehow, most people seemed to believe that.

'People who don't love children can be hard. If you ever hear what Miss Chin said about those two little girls that Mrs Chambers have.'

Miss Chin had one child, her daughter Pinky, who was not really her daughter, at least that is what other people said. They said Pinky was really the daughter of Miss Chin's sister who was bad, and had given birth to Pinky while she was still a schoolgirl.

We never knew what the real story was, but she held up Pinky as a symbol of purity and goodness in the Chinese tradition. You see Pinky there (concluding passage in today's homily on the sins of Miss Iris's daughter Cherry, who was spotted by Miss Chin laughing uproariously at the antics of drunken Valbert as he danced the yank to the tune of Fats Domino's 'Ahma going to the river, jump over-board and drown', outside Mr Albert's bar).

'Pinky never even look through the window when she hear all them kind of things going on you know. All them kind of rag song don't interest her. When she come home from school, she just go upstairs and you don't hear a sound from her. Sometimes I have to call her and say, "Pinky come down and rest your eyes, I don't want to have to buy glasses for you while you so young." I tell you, we know how to raise children properly, man.'

The truster nods . . . and says something like, 'Well fancy that eh . . . the little girl have ambition.' Miss Chin did not like me. She said, 'Puss bruk coconut in that little girl eye'. That was the most she ever said about me that I heard. I heard this because my friend Bev heard her telling this to Bev's Aunt Dolly, and naturally Bev told me. I told my mother who was furious. She said, 'You know I never think badly of other people's children,' and she pumped furiously at her sewing machine.

One day I heard the girls in the sewing room talking. Edith, my favourite of all the girls my mother taught to sew, said to Janette, a girl who always wore a man's hat (she did this to show his other girlfriends that she was the one he lived with) . . . said

'Guess who fall?' Janette running the pinking shears down the seam of a dress and leaving a row of pointed teeth along the seam said, 'Who?' Edith said, 'Pinky.' Janette dropped the garment she was finishing and screamed, 'You lie!.'

Pinky the perfect was quite pregnant. She had suddenly disappeared from the rooms above the shop and according to Miss Olive, the lady who worked for Miss Chin and Mr Chin, it was not even Miss Chin who had found out. It seemed Pinky had confessed her terrible secret to Mr Chin. The women of the area were appalled that Miss Chin did not as they all did, check upon their daughter's monthly health. For it seemed that Pinky was almost four months pregnant by the time the whole story came to light.

Four months pregnant by, of all people, Black Boy: the young man who swept out the shop and did all the dirty work, like chopping up the saltfish and the corn pork. In a way it was not difficult to understand. It must have been unbearably lonely for her up there in her castle above the shop with no one good enough to be her friend . . . Pinky fall. I knew exactly what my mother was going to say when she heard this.

Follow Your Mind

'But, Gatta, mi no have no church frock can fit mi, yu don't see how mi get big quick and furthermore even if mi can find a frock me can't find no hat fi wear.' 'Lawd, missis, nobody don't wear hat go a church again.' 'That a inna town, me no fully used to town ways yet . . . but Lord what I going to do though, eh?'

Sylvie folded her hands over her belly which rose full before her from her lap; she was six months pregnant. Lying-in fee, baby clothes, rent money, food . . . money, money for all these things, all her needs started chasing round and round in her head till they kicked up something like a dust cloud of anxiety which filled up her whole head . . . she didn't hear when Gatta said, 'Listen to me no. Every week down at Brother Sam Church, them feed people outta the Big Dutch pot wey them get from foreign. Me hear say the Dutch pot don't have no bottom, all one thousand people can get food outta it. Sometime dem give away clothes and things from foreign too, so you mighta all get some baby things.'

'Yes, but what me haffi do fi get that?'

'Nothing, you just join the church and go every now and again.'

Sylvie didn't like that. In the country where she came from, she went to church every Sunday, willingly, as a matter of fact she loved going to church and she really didn't feel sure that this plan that Gatta was putting forward was not some kind of sin. . . she wasn't sure what sin it was but it didn't sound right to her. To just go and join a church so, so you could get food and maybe some used clothes. You should join a church because you wanted to go there and worship God, at least that is what Sylvie believed.

'Boy, just through circumstances eh, just through a person can't do any better.' Up until four months ago Sylvie was an extremely contented woman. She and George living so good in the little room in the Big yard. The room was like a palace to Sylvie. They had a bed, a dresser, and a little table and three chairs, 'One fi visitor,' George had said. They also had a radio and Sylvie had planted mint and thyme and basil in paint pans which she had set outside the window. Sometimes in the before day morning she could smell the mint and the thyme and she maybe imagined that she was back in the country.

Many people had said that Sylvie had no ambition.

She was such a pretty girl with her smooth sambo colouring, and her dark ackee seed eyes, Sylvie with the black gums and the pretty teeth, only one thing though, her head dry. She had been so glad when low afros came into style and George said, 'But Sylvie, you was always my soul girl.'

People always said that Sylvie could have gotten somebody who was much better than George. Big, black, cheerful George. George head never make to take education so it was clear to everyone that he was not going to be any big shot because he had neither brains nor an aptitude for wrong doing. But Sylvie mind did just tell her that George was the man for her. Her soul and his just rest easy amongst one another. Sylvie trusted George and George trusted Sylvie and he knew how to make her laugh and to anticipate her needs and she did the same thing for him and they both wanted the same thing, some children and a farm in the country because anything George put his hand to it grow. George had to leave country and come to town though, because him just couldn't get a start, he wanted to lease a piece of land, so he figured if he could come to town and work and save some money, one day soon they could 'make life'. So George went to Kingston to live with his aunt till he found a job working in the Botanical Gardens.

Sylvie lived in misery till he sent for her. He sent a message by truck man (George no too inna the writing business) to say he had paid her fare, he had rented a room and would she just come and join him. Sylvie felt in her mind and soul that this was the right thing to do, so she went to join George in Kingston.

The bus stopped at Haywood Street market and Sylvie was quite frightened when she saw all the cars and buses and trucks and handcarts and what seemed like thousands of people in the streets. There were more people in this one street than there were in her entire village. Country people called Kingston, 'Killsome,' and it was a place that had killed some people in its time. Sylvie looked through the truck window anxiously for signs of George . . . and there standing up right beside a coconut cart she saw him, in a nice shirt that she had never seen before and her mind and her heart just went out across the congested market square to him. She felt sure she had done the right thing by coming to join him. George greeted her by holding her around her waist, 'Come here fat girl make we make haste and go home, I just dying to romance you . . .'

'Shhh George, mind the people dem hear.'

'Make them hear no, me no care . . . chuh you hear that Sylvie, me come a town come tun Deejay you know, coulda cut a chune, "Make them hear, for me no care," me say is you me really check for mi dear . . . gwan.' And Sylvie was laughing and laughing as George put down her suitcase in the middle of the street and was skanking like a man who felt that life was fine, a man in love, with his love close at hand and a quiet place to go and plenty of time. Make them hear, for me no care, me say is you me really check for mi dear . . .

When she woke up next morning she tried to figure out where she was, the room was so unfamiliar, George was not in the bed. He was sitting quietly over by the table by the window, 'Mi did fraid you wouldn't wake up.'

'So what you think mi did dead?'

'All right no mine. Come eat, I make breakfast fi you, but since is dinnertime now you better eat you dinner too . . .'

He looked at her so tenderly, then he said, 'Sylvie, fun and joke aside, mi glad you come fi stay with me. Mi glad you come fi stay with me.'

'Oh God, if George was here now yu see . . .'

'It no make no sense you fret bout George now, where him deh him can't help yu. Where him is?'

George in the Lockup. Police lock up George; flying squad move through the area one night and pick up nearly fifty men. George was standing on the sidewalk drinking a beer and them just scrape him up with everybody. Later on they say them holding him for questioning, say him look like a criminal bwoy name 'Country' who wanted for robbery with aggravation. George? Robbery with aggravation! George in a central Lockup without bail fi months now. You know say sometime man spend all two years inna Lockup before them charge them, Jesus have mercy. You know what go on inna them place dey? You know George real crime? Him poor and him no know no politician.

Sylvie went down to Central Police station nearly everyday to see George. The women in the yard were well acquainted with the prison runnings so they told her what to do. George told her to go back to the country. She said she was not leaving till he came out and then the two of them would go back to the country.

'I not leaving you George, I not leaving you.' Besides, by then she was pregnant.

'Come go with me Sunday.'

Sylvie thought about it and thought about it, what choice did she have. Up until recently she had a few days domestic work, but the bigger her belly grew the more difficult work became. Her mind did not feel so good about going to church in the hope that she would get some food and clothes, but what choice did she have?

'All right, it look like me wi haffi go wid yu.'

The Hallelujah temple was a big concrete church, that was designed to look like a dove with wings outstretched and praying hands at the same time. The Reverend Sam Phillips was a man of middle height with a pot belly and a balding head. When he opened his mouth to speak, he had a voice that needed no microphone to reach across considerable distance. Reverend Sam, as he was called, was a man who believed in the authority of those in high places. He believed that the servant should obey his master, he believed that to be rebellious was the worst possible sin. Furthermore, he believed that to be poor was as a result of some sin, passed down from generation to generation. He had been born poor and he was no longer poor. He had been redeemed; he was a righteous man.

Sylvie could not bring herself to go into church without a hat. So she tied her head with a clean, pretty headscarf and put on her best dress which by now was far too tight for her. The hem rode up in front hoisted by her belly and she was very uncomfortable as the zip could barely close up in the back. She took her Bible, and she walked with Gatta down to the Hallelujah temple. They were early, and Gatta walked right down to the front of the church and made to sit down. 'No Gatta, make we sit down in the back.'

'Then how them going see we, if we sit down in the back?'

Reluctantly, Sylvie sat in the front row and she just felt so out of place and so conspicuous.

The members of the congregation began to file in and fill up the seats; they were mostly very well-dressed people. Sylvie's unease started to grow, she started thinking about her little church in the country where everybody knew everybody else. She wished she was back in the country right now, she and George. Oh God George! Sylvie began to rock back and forth as she thought about George, clasping her belly bottom, for that was where she felt all her grief. Sylvie was rocking back and forth when Gatta hissed, 'Sylvie, is what wrong with you?'

Sylvie stopped . . . and tried to sit still, her shoulders hunched over in some sort of attempt to look inconspicious.

The service was about to begin. Reverend Sam was preceded into the church by the choir singing in good voice, he was accompanied by two visiting foreign evangelists. When it was time to pray, Sylvie could not kneel as her dress was too tight. As it was binding across her stomach, she stayed hunched over, hoping that the fact that she was not kneeling was not too obvious. Reverend Sam welcomed the visiting evangelists and said that they had come to hold a crusade and he hoped everyone would come to hear the words of God as spoken by these ambassadors for truth and democracy (he pronounced it demo-crassy). The visiting preachers stood up and brought greetings from the church overseas and said how glad they were to be visiting this beautiful island where the people were so in need of God's words.

The service proceeded and then it was time for the sermon. Sylvie did not know why, but even when she closed her eyes to pray she felt conspicious. At some point she began to feel that Reverend Sam was staring at her. Of course when she opened her eyes he was looking straight ahead of him. It was time for the sermon and Rev. Sam ascended to the pulpit, he paused dramatically and clutched the sides of the pulpit. And he began to preach in a voice that was very loud. He began his sermon with a personal testimony of how God had called him out of sin and shame, 'to serve him'. How he had been called to preach the gospel of repentance to sinners and how he had been doing that ever since that day he was called.

Reverend Sam then moved into the body of his sermon which was titled 'God helps those who help themselves.' It was a sermon in keeping with a speech made by a prominent politician that same week about the danger of a welfare state. That people were not to be encouraged to look to others for charity or to the state for handouts, that they were to pull themselves up by their bootstraps. 'It has come to me, brothers and sisters, that some people don't seem to want to help themselves, and even the smallest child know that God helps those who help themselves.'

Sylvie felt a burning begin in her body, it started in her ears and spread across her face and moved down till it seemed to settle in her belly.

Rev. Sam said, 'Take this business of having children without a plan.' Sylvie just knew he was looking at her right at this point, she just knew it.

'Some of us brothers and sisters don't even think about how we are going to feed and clothe these young ones before we bring them into the world, not a thought do we give for them, we just think of our own pleasure.'

Now Sylvie began to feel that all eyes in the church were directed at her belly. Sylvie sat there feeling really ashamed that she had allowed Gatta to force her to go against her feelings. She knew she should not have come to this place. Sylvie was feeling very ashamed and she was also feeling angry. Angry because she did not follow her mind. It was something her grandmother always said to her, 'Sylvie, follow your mind, woman especially must follow them mind.' Well right now, Sylvie's mind was giving her to walk out of this church right now. For no matter how things were bad with her, she could still see the lack of grace in Reverend Sam's sermon. After all, everybody's circumstances was different. It was true that God helped those who helped themselves, but because he was God, he really helped those who could not help themselves.

Reverend Sam then declared that because he was a man of God he was still going to give to the needy at this point in the proceedings. But that people would do well to remember that God helped those who helped themselves.

The rebuff within the sermon seemed to have gone over Gatta's head, because all she was thinking of is how hungry she was; but Sylvie was now just vexed. Gatta jumped up first when it was announced that the needy should stand in line.

'Come on, Sylvie.'

'I not going.'

'What you mean yu not going?'

People started to look at them. In order to avoid making a scene, Sylvie got up and joined the line with Gatta, but by then she knew exactly what she was going to do.

Reverend Sam was handing out food and clothing parcels to a long line of the needy. He was attended by the two visiting evangelists who first handed him the food and old clothes parcels, then he presented them to the needy with a whispered word, the needy accepted with grateful thanks.

When it came to Sylvie's turn it appeared that Rev. Sam had been waiting for her, as he stretched out his hand with the parcel he said loudly, 'Remember, God helps those who help themselves.' Sylvie just bit her lip and shook her head. He motioned to her to take the parcels and she said, 'I don't want it.' In order not to create a scene Reverend Sam turned to the needy directly behind Sylvie, and Sylvie just kept going, straight out of the church, because her mind was telling her that George was going to be out of Lockup very soon and that the two of them were going to be going to the country, and that in future she really was going to always try and follow her mind.

I Don't Want to Go Home in the Dark

He said on the telephone, 'I'm coming to get you.' He had arrived about forty-five minutes later, in his Quink-ink coloured, high-powered German vehicle. He was dressed in a light flannel shirt, designer jeans and very expensive-looking sneakers. He was a big man, with a moustache; he had a latin-lover look like an old-time movie star. He was very handsome. She thought him too handsome. He said, 'I told you I was coming to get you . . . bring a wrap or a jacket, we're going for a drive up into the hills.'

She liked going up into the hills . . . the higher you climbed, the more the vegetation became interesting: all sorts of temperate-looking flowers in muted colours, feathery inflorescence and insects not seen below where it was too hot for them to live. Once she'd been buzzed by an iridescent green bug with cellophane-like wings piped in darker green so the wings looked like window panes. Driving up into the hills it got cooler the higher you went, and you could almost imagine you were going for a drive in some foreign country . . . like you were in a novel, '. . . and towards evening they drove into an inn for supper'.

Once they were seated in the big car with the real-leather upholstered seats, he began to talk. He talked as if he had stored up everything he had to tell her for a long time, like he was just waiting to see her, to press his release button . . . she realized that all she had to do was to sit there and maybe say mmmmm every now and again.

Once she realized this, she did what she could do so very well. She slipped out of herself and hoisted herself up on to the roof of the car. It was a great advance view from up there. She could see way ahead of him into the oncoming distance, see the scoops in the road . . . the rises approaching and into the rooms of houses; also the wind filled her hair like many whispers and she laughed out loud and rolled from side to side every time the car dipped into a hollow. She thought about sitting right up on the bonnet, right where the silver emblem rode flagship on the front of the bonnet . . . it was at best a peace symbol within a circle, but peace should go with freedom and ought not be contained in a circle. She decided she was better off upon the roof. Eventually it was time to go back into herself, so she wiggled carefully through the window and re-entered, just in time, for he said just then . . . finally . . . 'So how have you been?' She smiled. He took that for an answer and then he continued, 'Anyway, there is a farm up ahead, I've put in two hundred acres and I'm hoping to buy eighty more.' The big car cleared the gateway and hummed to a stop inside the yard. There were about ten men standing in the driveway waiting for him. They all greeted him by crowding around the car and repeating his name over and over. She watched him turn into 'Landowner' right before her eyes . . . a big landowner. He used a different tone when he spoke to the workers. He was firm and authoritative and was something of a bully. He didn't introduce her, and she stood slightly apart from him wondering what to do with herself. She decided to sit on an ornate white garden bench out in the yard and from there to slip out of herself and go walking around the garden. She turned the corner away from where he was asking the workers about the progress of the money trees. 'How many notebuds did you put in?' 'Did they get enough water?' 'No I don't think that is a good enough answer.' She noticed a pregnant cat lying on its side under an azalea bush. The cat was resting like a fallen-from-grace beauty queen . . . her belly high with kittens. It was a touching and lovely sight but what was more exciting was that the azalea bush, shading the cat, was not alone.

It was part of a whole hedge. As a matter of fact, the entire yard was bordered by azalea bushes. Can you imagine how glorious that was going to be when they bloomed? There are few things lovelier than azaleas in a clay pot shimmering. He couldn't be so bad after all if he had the good taste to have a yard bordered by azaleas.

She felt that it was time to return. She was right, for as she got back to herself he said, 'It's a good thing you are such a dreamer . . . you can wait for long periods of time on other people while you dream.' She smiled. He said, 'Come let's go into the house.' She followed him as he took her on a tour of a house which was decorated just right (for some people). But she kept looking around for some spare love lying accidentally somewhere, a kiss left languidly on a smooth surface. Some spare love. She didn't see any. And then there was this magnificent candle holder containing clean candles. And she couldn't help herself, she said, 'I like candles which have burnt . . . you know? Candles with dripped wings at the sides.' He said, 'What?'

They sit in the living-room, there is a fire-place and she sits close to it . . . her seat is also near the door.

He sits or rather half-lies across a couch, the upholstery of which complements his shirt very well and he just looks very handsome, half-lying on that couch. Then he speaks . . . he gives her warning that he is about to speak and then he says, 'Please don't say anything until I have finished.' So she lets him speak. He explains that he finds himself thinking about her a lot at the most inconvenient times and things she says linger in his mind long after she has said them. The truth is he doesn't really have much time in his life for 'something like this' but he wants it. He is an important person, he can afford a lot of things: take this money farm for example, he plans to buy eighty acres of the land adjoining and put in more and more cash suckers and notebuds. She looks sleepy. He quickly says, 'Anyway you get the point of what I'm saying.' He says he knows he can't buy something like what he feels with her . . . for her . . . He knows, but right now, is there anything that she needs? Can he get her anything? And she says, 'Yes, azaleas.' And he says, 'What do you mean, azaleas?' And she says, 'Do you know that your whole yard is bordered by an azalea hedge? That's wonderful! And maybe when they bloom, you could bring me some azaleas, you know . . . like a lot of them. Maybe?'

He said, 'What the hell do you mean? I'm trying to be serious, can't you be serious just once. You drive a ten-year-old car and you live in a flat which is very charming but you don't own it and it might fall on your head soon and you are asking me for azaleas?'

She says, 'Yes.'

He gets really angry. He says, 'I always get what I want, you know.' She says, 'You probably do. Now can you take me home? I don't want to go home in the dark.'

On the way down, he drives very fast so she thinks it's not wise to go outside and sit on the bonnet, he turns the radio on and they are playing some really anonymous music. Usually she can identify songs like ten songs back after they've been played, this time she can't remember which song went before the white bread type one that was now playing. He doesn't speak.

She had hoped he would have stopped and cut some of the temperate looking flowers for her to take home. He does not. She thinks maybe she will just go home and bathe with a soap called *Wild Flowers* . . . it smelled exactly like mountain flowers and it would balance out the smell of the notebuds and his anger.

A Wise Man

Kane, when I first saw you, I knew I loved you. I was four years old, you were four years and three months and we had both come to school for the first time. You were always slim and not too tall for your age and you had angel's eyes. I guess I've always known there were black angels. You looked right into me and I saw you and I said, 'My friend?' and you said, 'My friend.' Yours was the statement, I always questioned. So we held hands and walked and skipped . . . walk a few steps, skip, walk for a longer time, skip, walk, skip, walk, skip . . . skip. And we always skipped in sync. And the sharing. One day you gave me a mango, so then you had none, so we shared it. And we had no knife to cut it so we each took a bite till we came to the seed. Then we took turns sucking the seed till it was almost white and all the golden juice and flesh had been shared between us. Then we put the seed in the sun to dry and we played till it got dry enough to draw a face on it. I took it first, and drew a woman's face and smoothed the hair into an upsweep. Then you took it and on the other side, you drew a man's face, made a moustache and smoothed the hair into a beard . . . Then you said, 'When I grow big, I'm going to have a beard' . . . and I said, 'Like a rasta?' and you said, 'Like a wise man.'

Kane, I always loved you. When we played dolly house and doctor and nurse and mother and father.

We lived in the same yard, and I'd get embarrassed when you saw me carrying the chamber pot downstairs into the toilet to empty it, and walk across the yard to the cistern to wash it. That was my morning duty, and you would always be sweeping the small verandah in front of the room you shared with your mother.

And I was always too embarrassed because you'd see me, so I pretended I didn't see you first thing in the morning. I'd only speak to you later when I descended into the yard for the second time from my family's rooms upstairs. I'd pretend I was seeing you for the first time that day, and I'd say, 'Hey boy, you never see me yet? If you see me again you will know me?' and you would say something like, 'How you see me looking at you if you wasn't looking at me?'

One day we had both broken our slates at school, so we walked home clutching the broken slates and the now useless wooden frames. I said, 'Your mother going to beat you?' and you said, 'Yes, but I don't fraid for beating.' Then you asked if my mother was going to beat me and I said, 'No,' (she was going to) then we started to sing, 'Chappa chappa slate gimme quattie bun, chappa chappa slate gimme quattie bun' until Miss B. passed and said, 'This little girl love boy company see,' and for the first time I began to think that there might be something wrong with loving you.

My mother soon after that began to tell me that I was a big miss and that I should not run up and down so much, that I should not 'sit down bad' and that I should try to play with the girls some more.

They also started to tell me what a nice looking little girl I was, that I had good hair and how the only thing that spoiled my face was my nose (which is big and flat), but that if I pinched it up every morning between my thumb and forefinger, that action would help build up a nose bridge. Then I'd be perfect and maybe I'd marry some important somebody one day and go to live up in St Andrew in a big house.

Kane, do you remember one day we were standing side by side at the window in the 'hall' up in my house? It had been raining heavily and we were watching the dark brown, like hot chocolate tea water rolling down the gully bed. We used to stand for a long time and watch this dirty urban river bearing all manner of refuse . . . sweeping down the gully bed. The tin cans would play a great noisy symphony as they beat against the stones and scraped the bottom of the concrete gully bed.

Sometimes there would be dead animals floating in the water, and then I'd duck down and hide and ask you from below the window sill, 'The dead dog gone yet?' and you'd say, 'Yes' . . . but sometimes that was not true, and when I looked out and saw the awful carcass floating by I'd scream and duck down again and you would laugh. Do you remember that day we were standing side by side at the window watching the water and you just reached across and pulled me to you so that we stood close, close, shoulder to shoulder, thigh to thigh and your ankle and mine pressed sharp into each other like we were Siamese twins, Kane, my being then acknowledged that joining as that of my twin, my soul's self . . . and thereafter, through all the times when I was under the spell of other hands, I always knew that those hands were not yours and therefore not right.

When I became a 'woman' they told me that I definitely should stay away from you. That I should no longer play with you because now I could be a mother. That I should concentrate upon studying my lessons, so that I could pass my exams and get a good job and move up into society. One day on the bus coming home from school, you sat beside me and we talked about school things, 'But algebra is so easy'; 'I don't like Latin either'. We were now so tense with each other. I got up and moved ahead of you as we still came off the same stop . . . and you said, 'Walk slowly, I'll walk behind you, your skirt stain up,' and you walked behind, covered me from behind till we reached my gate . . . . . . covered for me as we walked past the boys on the bridge who said, 'See Kane, hitch up under you frock tail though.'

Then you got a girl friend. I was not allowed to have boy friends, and I hated her, because her mother was very happy that you were keeping company with her. One day, again on the bus, I said to you, 'Is she your girl friend?' and you said, 'Some sort of a way' . . . and then (you always knew how to claim me) you said, 'But you know it's me and you, and you'll never forget me . . . I will walk up and down inside your head.' You said that, and we were only fifteen then, and I started to cry right there on the bus.

You told me, Kane, you told me, how you knew they felt you

were not good enough for me. Your mother sell in the market . . . my mother and father own the yard.

Then we moved, and we only saw each other every once in a while. One night I went with my St Andrew friends (my family had finally made the Jump to the class above), I went with my St Andrew friends to hear merritime disco. My friends and I went because it was 'the thing' to do, and you were there dancing with a stout slow girl . . . and you could always dance . . . and you danced past me and looked into my face . . . and said, 'Good evening.'

Then you looked at the pretty brown boy I was dancing with and just shook your head. And I said something like, 'Hi' . . . and we just danced past each other like we were Sarah Vaughan and Billy Eckstine . . . 'Play passing strangers now Merri.'

Kane, how did you feel when you heard that I married my big important politician husband, my big important husband with his big house on Pineapple Heights, my big conservative husband who hates our music? How did you feel when you realized that I believed what they told me . . . that you were not good enough for me.

How did you feel when you heard I was pregnant? What did you think when I had a daughter? Then another. You always said you wanted daughters. When we played dolly house, you always wanted daughters more than you wanted sons.

Kane, the little girl who drew the lady on the mango seed has gone deep into hiding.

One day recently I saw you in the traffic . . . you were driving a car that was a deep dark green like a forest . . . like the deep dark green of abundance. You had the window rolled down and you were rocking back and forth in your seat to a strong reggae rhythm.

'It's hard to confess to a love that's strong.'

I had my tinted glass rolled down for once. I could see you and feel you and one of my daughters said, 'Mummy, why are you looking over at that rasta man . . .' (you do have a beard . . . you do look like a wise man). Then she said, 'And mummy, what are you crying for?'

The Big Shot

Albert woke up drenched with sweat, his own heart about to attack him in his chest, the same horrible, dreadful dream again.

The dream in which he was walking through his old neighbourhood, through West Kingston, past the broken-down houses and the many-roomed Government yards, walking past the knots of criminals (everybody there looked like a criminal to him) standing on the street corners, the leaning zinc fences that barely concealed all manner of nameless horrors waiting to jump out and claim him. 'Albert, is you that star? Chuh is when you come forward . . . let off a munney no. You see Delzie and the youth yet?' The older ones would heap blessings on him and remind him and remind him of the more embarrassing moments of his childhood. 'You see him there, me used to change him nappy you know!'

This dream wouldn't leave him, even after so many years. He was now way past those circumstances and those people, but the dream wouldn't leave him. Even as a child he hated the poverty and looked down on the poor people around him. He was going to get out as soon as he could. He always knew this. He was bright, so much more intelligent than all the other children at his school.

He never knew his father: some people said his mother had had him with a university professor for whom she used to do domestic work. Albert grew up with his granny, Miss Cordy. When he had passed his Common Entrance Examinations they had come to congratulate her. 'Him is a brains, Miss Cordy, mus be all the fish head you give him . . . God bless him.' Miss Cordy accepted the praise, 'Ah my love, the Good Lord help to carry him through, him say him want to go for lawyer nuh.'

In the one room where Albert lived with his granny, Albert was a Prince. Miss Cordy sold fruits and sweets and fritters to the children at the school gate in order for Albert to dress better and eat better than all the other children. Miss Cordy always wore one of two dresses; then she had a white dress for going to church and a pair of good shoes and a hat and precious little else.

Albert and his grandmother slept in the same bed in the little room with the board floor that was always shining. Then there was a small table with two chairs and an old wooden press in which Albert and Miss Cordy's clothes were hung.

Albert's mother did not live in Kingston, she lived in Montego Bay where it was said she worked in a 'sport house'. Sometimes she would send him a card at Christmas with a little money in it, but for the most part it seemed that she had abandoned his upbringing to Miss Cordy. Miss Cordy's aim in life was for Albert to become a lawyer, and Albert's aim was to move as far away from the poverty and poor people in West Kingdom as was possible.

Albert got up out of bed, Prudence, his wife, was fast asleep, 'dead to the world' as his grandmother would have said. Sometimes he was amazed at how Miss Cordy spoke through him, although he made a point of never speaking 'broken English'. Sometimes he could hear himself thinking like her. He went into the kitchen, he particularly liked the kitchen of this house, it was big and cheerful with bright curtains and every imaginable electrical appliance; it looked like a kitchen in *Splendid Homes and Magnificent Gardens*. That is exactly how he wanted it, and that is the look the interior decorator had achieved. He sat in the breakfast nook sipping a cup of brandy and hot milk, trying to soothe himself back to sleep.

He really liked this kitchen, sometimes he thought about the dreadful, dark, narrow little lean-to they referred to as a kitchen in the yard where he had lived with his grandmother. Once or twice when Miss Cordy was sick he had to go into the kitchen to cook . . . the fire wall was black and furry with soot and you had to look for chips of wood all over the yard to help 'catch up' the coal fire. Actually, making a fire was something Albert used to get very absorbed in doing. He would fill the bowl of the small cast iron stove with coals, having raked out the ashes from the previous meal's cooking. Then he'd put the small chips of wood criss-crossing each other in the centre of the bed of coal. Next he'd roll up bits of newspaper which he'd carefully wedge under the arrangement of chips. A little kerosene oil poured over the chips and a match to light it. At first the flame would shoot straight up and you had to be careful if you were bending over the stove. The flame soon died down and then the chips would burn down to conduct fire into the coals. You had to keep fanning the fire awhile with a piece of cardboard or an old almanac or even a piece of tin, like the lid of a kerosene tin that was used to boil white clothes.

Albert was a very methodical person and he remembered every detail of lighting fires in the tenement yard kitchen. So when he inclined the knob of his big shining gas stove and the clean blue flame rose up as high or as low as he wanted it to go, his heart would rise too for he had made it. The dream usually flew the gate for bad memories. Hard on the heels of catching up the fire was of course remembering Delzie and the baby . . . the teenage child it would now be; the child she said was his.

Miss Cordy had called Albert into the room, he was sitting outside on a bench trying to read a book by the light of a bottle torch. He could have gone inside the room and read by the Home Sweet Home kerosene lamp, but sometimes he could not abide the physical closeness with his grandmother, her old lady smell . . . and he was avoiding her because he was in trouble. 'Yes Granny?'

'Albert, is true say Delzie pregnant and she call your name?' He stood before his grandmother with his head held down, his face burning with shame . . . 'Yes, mam.'

'Well, since you done pass out your exam and we done decide say you going to England already, just as cheap you go right now. Me never bring you so far fi throw away yourself pon a little black girl like Delzie' . . . and the move was decided as simply as that.

Albert and his granny kept a conspiracy of silence. Nobody in the yard or the neighbourhood knew when he left for England. No cars filled with well-wishers had gone to the airport to see him off. No friends and relatives stood on the waving gallery to wave at him until he disappeared inside the plane. He left before Delzie became obviously pregnant, so he never even saw her with her belly. Back in those days he used to wonder who the child would look like, would it be a boy or girl . . .then he stopped wondering and came to the conclusion that none of that had any bearing on him or his life.

About six months after he reached London and was beginning to be settled in the English life, he received a letter from his mother.

Dear Son,

I regret to tell you that your grandmother take sick and now she is gone to a silent home. I had was to come to town and bury her. All her thoughts was of you. Please don't forget to remember me, study hard and make yourself into real big shot.

Your loving mother,

Cherrylin Brown.

Albert stayed in his room for days crying for Miss Cordy, the only person he had ever really loved, who loved him more than herself. As for his mother, he never wrote to her again after he sent her £5 towards 'Expenses'.

Albert became used to the English way of life very easily. It was as if all the time he had been in rehearsal for a move up to a higher quality life-style. He studied hard and did well at his exams and went out with a number of English girls who found him very attractive. The one woman he would like to have married was Jane. Big, blonde, pretty Jane who seemed to laugh all the time and thought that life should not be taken seriously. When he suggested marriage to her, Jane giggled, 'Oh love, my parents would die of mortification, I'm going to have to marry some boring Englishman, one day. So for now why don't we just have a wonderful time?' And they did. But Albert needed a wife. It was time for him to go home to Jamaica. Much as he liked Britain he knew the chances of him making it really big in his field in England were slim. Albert was not a fool, when he looked in the mirror he saw himself. He was a slim, very elegant, light brown man and although his nose was straight enough and his lips were not too thick and his hair was cut low enough to look not so kinky . . . he was not a white man.

He married Prudence, a nurse. Prudent in every way. From the beginning of the marriage she took over the running of their finances and they were able to arrive in Jamaica with enough money to set up a practice downtown where all established lawyers were located. Prudence found a job at a private hospital and their joint incomes enabled them to buy a fine house in Cherry Blossom Gardens. He never visited the old neighbourhood and sometimes when he met somebody he used to know from his childhood he'd become very formal and very busy. 'Yes, I'm Albert Stephenson, what's your name again . . . right. Well it was good to see you,' and he moves off before they can beg for money or a favour. They didn't have any children though and once Prue had suggested that they adopt a Jamaican child and he looked at her very coldly.

Albert easily moved into the tennis-playing, smart, middle-class, Benz-driving set and his taste for fine clothes made him look like what Miss Cordy and his mother wanted him to be. He was a qualified big shot. Life was mostly great except for the dream. Albert went back to bed soothed by the brandy and dreamt he was made a High Court Judge.

One day the air-conditioning in his car had broken down so the drive down was hot. He asked his secretary to bring him a cold beer from the refrigerator, when he looks at his papers on his desk he finds a message that a Miss Hyacinth Goodman had called to speak to him. Probably some market woman with her son in the gun court.

He sits down at his desk and the secretary calls in to say Miss Goodman had returned and could he see her . . . He says yes, and in walked Delzie. The damn stupid habit which ignorant Jamaican people have of calling people by a 'pet' name. A 'pet' name which often had absolutely no connection with their real name!

Standing before him was Delzie; older, fatter with her side teeth missing but unmistakably Delzie. Her eyes had not changed much, she was still good-looking in an honest, simple kind of way. She looked right into his face when she spoke to him. He looked up at her and said, 'Yes?' She said, 'Albert, you don't remember me?' He said, 'Yes, what can I do for you?' She stood there just looking at him listening to his very English-sounding voice. She remembered how they used to joke with each other innocently, until the night his grandmother had gone to church and he invited her into their room so that he could 'show her something', and she liked him so much that she had gone with him. She was only sixteen years old then.

After Albert had run off to England leaving her with 'the belly', Delzie's young life had gone to hell.

She had been forced to go and live with her aunt in the East end of Kingston, because her parents were church-going people and they were so ashamed that she had brought scandal upon their name. Her aunt was a very respectable woman who was glad to take in the fallen girl, only she always reminded Delzie how much she was doing for her, and it was felt that she gave her just a little too much to do around the house in exchange for her keep.

Delzie gave birth to Albert's son down at Victoria Jubilee hospital known as Lineen. She shared a bed with another teenaged mother who kept screaming terrible bad words. Delzie had listened to the other girl screaming and had sworn she would not behave like that. When her labour pains intensified she just loudly begged God to take her. When the child was born, her relatives asked her what his name was and she said, 'Albert Stephenson'. They had been so angry. 'Have sense. You don't see Albert gone leave you and the pickney, him don't want you or the child, so why you going to go and give it him name?' Delzie had remained silent and she had registered the child in the name of Albert Stephenson.

Standing in Albert's office, all of this came to her and when she saw the indifference on Albert's face, she thought maybe she should just walk out and leave. This really was a shameful relationship, one big negation of her humanity from beginning to end. But she finds her voice and says, 'I never come here to beg you anything, you know Albert, not a thing. For me know say retribution going to take care of you like how it take care of your grandmother.'

'So what brings you here then?'

'Your son.'

'My Son? Listen to me, I don't know anything about that. I suggest you find one of the other men in the neighbourhood to saddle with your problems.'

'Yes, your son, if you kill me dead, is your son. You could cut off mi neck, is your son, him is the dead stamp of you and you is the first man and only man me did take.'

'Would you lower your voice, this is an office.'

'Oh you feel I can't see that for myself? You know something, you really is a facety dirty dog . . . you could climb high little more, but you really sneaking and low, you know. You know I never come here this morning with the intention of having no fuss with you. Me forget bout you long time. But you son, yes you son . . . get involve and police hold him.

'I only come here this morning to see if outta your conscience you could do something to help him but you know something, I don't want anything from you . . . you see yourself, you look like a idiot, you hear yourself, "this his han hoffice", Gwey. Albert you confuse, when you fine you real self maybe you can help somebody. Right now you need help more than me. You is a real poppyshow.'

'Take you rass outta mi office,' Albert hears himself scream and reaching for the beer bottle breaks it on the edge of his desk . . . it was amazing how naturally the street-fighting ghetto persona overcame him, and the fact that he'd chosen to drink a cold beer after he'd come in out of the heat meant he had the symbolic ghetto weapon at hand. 'Take you rass otta mi office before I cut out you.' He heard himself screaming this after Delzie as she disappeared through the door.

For some reason Delzie was laughing as she hurried out of Albert's office. The fact that she and what she represented had been able to trigger off such a response in him somehow seemed like payment for all the years she had felt so hurt and rejected, but she also felt sorry for him, she couldn't say why. Before Delzie met Lynval, she used to think there was no justice in the world. Lynval was her husband, the father of her two daughters and her baby son.

Lynval had made her know just how good a relationship between a man and a woman could be. When she had become pregnant, for him a beautiful and tender scenario began to unfold between them. Lynval bringing her some special little sweet something to eat every evening. Lynval rubbing her big belly with baby oil. Lynval hurrying home to cook the dinner for the first month because the smell of cooking oil nauseated her, and she calling him 'Papa' and referring to him as 'The Baby Father' and she staying up late every night the week before she went to hospital to have the baby, washing and ironing all his clothes so that he could go to work clean and tidy while she was in the hospital. When she took in, in the middle of the night, Lynval went to wake up the taxi man who lived three streets away and held her in his arms all the way to Lineen.

Lynval was a much better man than Albert any day. Lynval had never treated her son, Albert, differently from their other children, but the boy had something of his father in him. Like he was always in a hurry, always want what their poor, but proud existence couldn't provide. The police had held him saying he was involved in housebreaking and larceny. Lynval was out looking bail for him. She never told him of her plan to go to Albert, his father, for help. She decided she would not tell him she had been.

Albert was no real father to his child. She and Lynval would just have to go on struggling with him. Besides, with all of Albert's big shot ways, he didn't look like somebody who had had a good night's sleep in a long time.

Albert's dream continued, but with a new dimension. He now walks into the old neighbourhood and the streets turn into a courtroom and he is the judge, and he calls the court to order. A young man with his face and his name is brought before him for murder.

Moon

Do you know that there is a connection between lovers and Chinese food?' He looks at her with his 'I can't believe this woman' look. 'What?' 'Yes, it's true. I've never been to a Chinese restaurant where there wasn't at least one pair of lovers somewhere in a corner eating while they ate each other with their eyes. Also, you can tell what is the state of the relationship by how they eat and how much they eat.'

He looks across at her and he can't help himself, but he is slightly annoyed. Her vagueness, her far-out ideas which he finds so endearing sometimes annoy him slightly, now. Sometimes, it's like she goes off on an ethereal journey and he is angry because he cannot go all the way with her. Like this lovers and Chinese food theory, it's interesting but he doesn't enter fully into it right away. Sometimes he misses the sensible down-to-earthness of the familiar woman.

If he were with her, they would probably be talking about ways to make money or they'd be discussing something that they had both read in today's newspaper. Sometimes it became very necessary to be around her, her familiarity was so reassuring; but the flip side of that was dull.

Moon (that was their private name for her), Moon, because she liked silvery things and her face was round and there were strong tides of feelings always flowing through her, Moon was something rare. He balanced both women skilfully, he thought, sometimes he was overawed at the amount of riches he possessed in them collectively.

Moon is smiling now, she bends over and is whispering to him, 'Look over there in that corner, do you see that couple?' He glances over and in the corner there is a man in his early fifties, looking like a business executive. He is with a slender young girl who looks like she could have recently joined his firm as a trainee in the marketing department.

The man is ordering from the menu in a confident and experienced way; the girl looks nervous but she is obviously also quite thrilled. The man is in charge, he says to the girl, 'I'm sure you will like Mushrooms in Oyster Sauce, trust me.' The girl nods and says, 'All right.'

The man is speaking a little too loudly, for his last remark hangs in the air, right up there with the fringed red paper lanterns. In spite of himself, David was drawn into the unfolding of the Lovers and Chinese Food Theory.

'You see,' says Moon, 'that's the early stages. They haven't been to bed together yet, the girl is not sure that she should, but she is responding favourably to his bold, masterful "take charge" attitude, she probably will give him her body, and that's the stage the relationship is at. Now later when they are lovers they won't take so much time ordering, they will have favourites by then.'

Then she said, 'What stage do you think our relationship is at?' (That's another thing about Moon, she resisted all rules, grammatically and otherwise.) David was such an organized businesslike type, he hardly ever used slang. He is unprepared for the question. 'What exactly do you mean by that?' he asks her. 'Think about it before you answer me, please,' says Moon. He finds her very endearing right now, she is very exotic looking, sort of Rasta Chic. Sometimes she was so otherworldly, he wonders if he could live with her every day, it would probably be like drinking champagne in the morning or eating lobster every Monday. Sometimes he saved her up, like he used to relish some particularly nice treat as a child; don't eat it right away, save it for a day or two then go to it with all your strength. She had brought a quality to his life he never expected to find, he had not really looked for it because he didn't know it. Like one midday he had returned to work for a meeting to find a telegram on his desk, it just said, 'Come – Moon.'

He had only just left her a few hours before, so he panicked and called her house. The phone just rang and rang. He was forced to cancel the meeting and dash around to her house . . . he arrived to find the front door open, he rushes in to find Moon sitting at the dining-table before a feast of fruit and wine, a fat bird-shaped bread as the centre piece and flowers and lit candles all around the room . . . he is stunned. She says, 'Today is the anniversary of the first time I ever saw you, you were boarding an Air Jamaica plane and I asked somebody what your name was and they said . . . forget it, he's not your type . . . this feast is to prove that they were wrong.' In spite of himself he is overwhelmed, thrilled, he feels a surge of happiness which almost lifts him off the ground . . . he just forgets about his meeting and allows himself to be drawn along by this very strong, powerful and refreshing tide. Sometimes he fears he will drown in one of them, but somehow he always emerges feeling like a new man.

He reaches across the table and holds her face between his hands, 'Why are you asking me this now, Moon?'

'Because you will have to choose, soon.'

'Choose? What do you mean?'

'No, you must not do that . . . you and I already know what we mean. I just think now is the time for choosing.'

He says, 'Look, you know I don't take ultimatums from *anybody*,' he stresses the anybody, because this turn in the evening has taken him completely by surprise, and he is angry at being caught off guard.

'Oh yes' she says, 'I know that, but this is not an ultimatum though, it's an invitation to choose. You can't have it all, sweetheart, that's greedy,' she giggles.'It's like trying to eat too much Chinese food, like that man over there.' She motions to the man in the corner, who in his zeal has ordered enough food for four people. She continues, 'Sometimes too much can make you fat and complacent. Aah, maybe I'm too strange for you anyway.' Her voice has become soft, soft. She is humming, and he looks across the table at her. It is very difficult for him to envisage what his life will be like without her, he thinks back to before her, and quickly comes forward. He says, 'I need time to think about this, you are right.' She stops humming, she says,

'OK, I'm going to be gone until you decide. I'm going away tomorrow afternoon.'

'And you are only just telling me this?'

'I anticipated your response, I'm even more knowing than you think.'

He just looks at her dumbfounded. That was another thing about her: people said she 'knew things', she denied that, but sometimes her 'intuition' was very accurate.

They fall silent now, then she takes out a small notepad and begins to read from a list. It's a list of all the arrangements she has put into place for her journey and for her plans to keep her affairs at home going while she is away. He is amazed at how organized and businesslike she sounds.

By Love Possessed

Sometimes, she used to wake up and just look at him lying asleep beside her, she would prop herself up on one elbow and study his face. He slept like a child, knees drawn up to his stomach, both hands tucked between his thighs. His mouth was always slightly open when he slept, and his mouth-water always left a damp patch on the pillowcase. No matter how many days after, it seem the patch would always be damp, and every time she washed it she would run her finger over the stain and her mind would pick up the signal and move back to the image of him lying asleep. When the radio next door began to play the first of the morning church services, she would know that it was time to begin to get ready to go to work. From Monday to Saturday, every day, her days began like this. She would go to the kitchen to prepare his breakfast, then she would leave it covered up on top of the stove over a bowl of hot water. Then she would go to the bathroom, bathe in the cold early morning water and then get dressed. Just before she left she always placed some money on the top of the bureau for his rum and cigarettes, then she would say to his sleeping form, 'Frenchie, ah gone, take care till I come back.'

Dottie sometimes wondered how she was so lucky to be actually living with Frenchie. He was easily the best-looking man in Jones Town, maybe in the whole of Jamaica and she, ten years older than him, tall and skinny and 'dry up'. She had never had luck with men and she had resigned herself to being an old maid a long time ago. She was childless, 'a mule', as really unkind people would say. She worked hard and saved her money, and she kept a good house. Her two rooms in the big yard were spotless. She had a big trunk bed that was always made up with pretty chenille spreads, a lovely mahogany bureau, a big wardrobe with good quality glass mirrors and in the front room, in pride of place, her China Cabinet. Nobody in the yard, maybe in Jones Town, maybe in the whole of Jamaica, had a China Cabinet so full of beautiful things. Dottie had carefully collected them over the years and she never used them. Once a year when she was fixing up her house at Christmas, she would carefully take them out, the ware plates, cups and saucers, tureens, glasses, lemonade sets, serving dishes and teapots, and she would carefully wash them. This took her nearly a whole morning. She washed them in a pan of soapy warm water, rinsed them in cold water, then dried them with a clean towel. Then she would rearrange them artistically in the Cabinet. On that night, she would sometimes treat herself to a little drink of Porto Pruno wine, sitting by herself in her little living room and would gaze on her China Cabinet enjoying the richness within, the pretty colours and the lights bouncing off the glasses. Her sister always said that she worshipped her possessions. Maybe she did, but what else did she have? Till she met Frenchie.

There was one other thing that Dottie really liked: she liked the movies, and that is how she met Frenchie. She was in the line outside the Ambassador theatre one Saturday night, waiting to get into a hot triple bill, when she struck up a conversation with him. He was standing in the line behind her and she remembered feeling so pleased that a man as good looking as this was talking to her. They moved up in the line till they got to the cashier, she being ahead of him, took out ten shillings to pay for herself. It was the easiest most natural thing in the world for her to offer to pay for him when he suddenly raised an alarm that his pocket had been picked. If she had been seeing straight, she would have noticed that some people were laughing when he raised the alarm. But she didn't see anything but the handsome brown-skin man with 'good hair', straight nose and a mouth like a woman's.

It was the best triple bill Dottie ever watched. He had walked her home. All the way home they talked about the movie. His favourite actor was Ricardo Montalban; she liked Delores Del Rio, for that is how she would like to have looked, sultry and

Spanish, for then she and Frenchie would make a striking couple, just like two movie stars. As it was, she looked something like Popeye's girlfriend Olive Oyl and he was probably better looking than Ricardo Montalban.

Frenchie did not work. He explained that he used to have a job at the wharf but he got laid-off when his back was damaged unloading some cargo. She sympathized with him and some nights she would rub the smooth expanse of his back with wintergreen oil. He said he liked how her hands felt strong. Frenchie moved in with Dottie about two weeks after they met. At first, she was a little shy about having a man living in her room, then she began to be very proud of it. At last she was just like any other woman in the yard. As a matter of fact, she was luckier than all of them, for Frenchie was so good looking. 'She mind him. Dottie buy down to the very drawers that Frenchie wear,' said her sister, 'not even a kerchief the man buy for himself.'

The people in the yard would laugh at her behind her back, they wondered if Frenchie kept women with her. Winston her nephew said, 'Chu, rum a Frenchie woman, man, you ever see that man hug up a rum bottle?'

Now that was true. Frenchie loved rum and rum loved him, for he never seemed to get drunk. As a matter of fact, every day he spent a good eight hours, like a man going to work, in Mr Percy's bar at the corner. After Dottie had gone to work at the St Andrew house where she did domestic work for some brown people, Frenchie would wake up. He would bathe, eat the breakfast that Dottie had left for him and get dressed, just like any man going to work. He always wore white short-sleeved shirts which Dottie washed whiter than 'pelican shit'; he favoured khaki pants, so she ironed both shirt and pants very carefully.

He would get dressed very, very carefully; put some green brilliantine in his hair and brush it till it had the texture of a zinc fence, or as one of the men in the yard said, 'Everytime I see you hair, Frenchie, I feel sea-sick.' Frenchie would laugh showing his gold crown on his front teeth, run his hand over his hair and say, 'Waves that behaves, bwoy, waves that behaves.'

When his toilette was over, he would walk leisurely up the road to the bar. The one thing which made you realize that he could not have been going to work like any other decent man was his shoes, he always wore backless bedroom slippers. Frenchie would sit in the bar and make pronouncements on matters ranging from the private life of the Royal Family (Princess Margaret was a favourite topic), to West Indian Cricket (he always had inside knowledge on these matters), general world affairs and most of all, the movies.

Everybody was in awe of Frenchie, he was just so tough, handsome and in control of life. His day at the bar usually ended at around five p.m., just like any other working man. Then he would walk home and join the Domino game which went on constantly in the yard. Usually Dottie would find him at the Domino table when she burst in through the gate, always in a hurry, anxious to come home and fix his dinner. She always said the same thing when she came through the gate, 'Papa, ah come,' and he, looking cool and aloof, eyes narrowed through the cigarette smoke, would say, 'Oh, yu come.'

Dottie always experienced a thrill when he said that, it was a signal of ownership, the slight menace in his voice was exciting, you know it gave her the right to say, 'Frenchie vex when I come home late . . .'

She would hurry to fix his dinner and set it on the table before him. She hardly ever ate with him, but sat at the table watching him eat. 'Every day Frenchie eat a Sunday dinner,' Winston would say. It was true, Dottie cooked only the best for Frenchie. He ate rice and peas at least three times per week unlike everybody else who only ate it on Sundays. Dottie would leave the peas soaking overnight and half boil them in the morning, so that they could finish cooking quickly when she hurried home in the evenings. He also had beef steak at least twice a week and 'quality fish' and chicken the rest of the week.

Dottie lived to please Frenchie. She was a character in a film, *By Love Possessed.* Then one day in Mr Myers' bar, the movies turned into real life. Frenchie was sitting with his usual group of drunkaready friends talking about a movie he had seen, when a stranger stepped into the saloon; actually he was an ordinary man.

He had a mean and menacing countenance because he was out of work and things were bad at home. He walked into the bar and ordered a white rum and sat on a bar stool scowling, screwing up his face every time he took a sip of the pure 100% proof cane spirit, and suddenly Frenchie's incessant talking began to bother the stranger; the more Frenchie talked, the more it bothered him. He looked at Frenchie's pretty boy face and his soft looking hands and he hated him.

Then Frenchie reached a high point of the story he was telling. He was painting a vivid picture of the hero, wronged by a man who doubted his integrity and Frenchie was really into it . . . he became the wronged hero before everyone's eyes, his voice trembled, his eyes widened in disbelief as the audience gazed spellbound at him. 'Then the star boy say,' said Frenchie, 'him say, "What kind of man do you think I am?"' The stranger at the bar never missed a beat . . . he replied, 'A batty man.' And the bar erupted. The laughter could be heard streets away. The barmaid laughed till they had to throw water on her to stop her from becoming hysterical. All the people who had ever wanted to laugh at Frenchie laughed at him. All the people who envied him his sweet-boy life, laughed at him. Everybody was laughing at him.

The uproar didn't die down for almost half an hour and people who heard came running in off the streets to find out what had happened. One man took it upon himself to tell all the newcomers the story, over and over again. Frenchie was sitting stunned, he tried to regain face by muttering that the man was a blasted fool . . . but nobody listened.

Finally, the self-appointed raconteur went over to him and said, 'Cho Frenchie, you can't take a joke?' Then he lowered his voice, taking advantage of the fallen hero and said, 'All the same yu know everybody must wonder bout you, how a good-looking man like you live with a mawgre dry up ooman like Dottie. She fava man, she so flat and crawny.' Upon hearing this, Frenchie got angrier, and funnily enough, he wasn't angry at the man, he was angry at Dottie. It was true, she didn't deserve him, she was mawgre and crawny and dry up and really was not a woman that a handsome, sexy man like should be with. No wonder the blasted ugly bwoy coulda facety with him. He understood what the hero meant in the movies when he said he saw red. Frenchie felt like he was drowning in a sea of blood . . . he wanted to kill Dottie! He got up and walked out of the bar to go home.

When Dottie hurried in through the door that evening, saying breathlessly, 'Papa, ah come,' she was met with the following sight: Frenchie standing at the door of her front room with her best soup tureen in one hand and four of her best gold-rimmed tumblers stacked inside each other in the other hand, and as soon as he saw her he flung them into the street. He went back inside and emerged with more of the precious things from her China Cabinet and he flung them into the street where they broke with a rich full sound on the asphalt. After a while, he developed a steady rhythm, he began to take what looked like the same amount of steps each time he went into the house, then he'd emerge with some crockery or glass, walk to the edge of the verandah taking the same amount of steps and with an underarm bowling action, fling the things into the street. Dottie screamed, she ran up the steps and clutched at him; he gave her a box which sent her flying down the steps. Everybody screamed. The men kept saying that he had gone rass mad . . . nobody tried to restrain him for he had murder in his eyes . . . and he never stopped till he had broken all of Dottie's things and then he walked out of the yard.

'Frenchie bad no rass bwoy. You see when him just fling the things, chuh.' Frenchie's name became a great legend in the neighbourhood, nobody had ever seen anybody 'mash it up' like that so; nobody had ever seen anybody in such a glorious temper 'mash up the place to blow wow'. Nobody remembered him for 'What kind of man do you think I am?' Even poor broken Dottie remembered him for his glorious temper. She would have forgiven him for breaking her precious things; she would like to have told the story of how bad her man was and the day he broke everything in her China Cabinet and boxed her down the steps. But he didn't give her a chance. She kept going to the Sunday night triple bills at the Ambassador, but she never saw him again, and after that she took a live-in job and gave up her rooms in the yard.

From The Clearing of Possibility

He said, 'For so many years I've been wanting to tell you that you are hope and beauty personified and I care so much about you, won't you just let me?' And she said, 'What about . . .?' And he said, 'That relationship is stagnant, and I'll die if I stay in it and I feel like you can give me life.' And she who had given up on love on earth yielded to his want and he drew from her, but always after dark. And then one day she saw him in daylight, in public, in a company of people they both knew . . . she walked towards him and his face went blank and he did not recognize her . . . he was also with the one who was indicated as the 'other' in the stagnant relationship. He drew closer to that one and left her isolated in the middle of the room on her way over to embrace him.

There must be a limit to how much hurt the human heart can accept, how much betrayal the spirit can take before it twists into something dark and poisonous . . . becomes the colour of a John Crow nosehole flower, the ugliest bloom ever. Or it leaves the body, separates itself from it . . . the spirit and the body part company and the body is left empty leaving room for terrible djinn to inhabit . . . that older woman making up a fire at the corner of Trafalgar Road . . . the girl washing her clothes at the pipe in the park – washing her one suit of clothes she is stark naked, she is hanging her panties on the barbed wire fence to the view of the morning traffic. Hurt cleaved them in two, a hurt so deep, so sharp, it cut them in two . . . that man sitting like a king in his sunken bath tub . . . that man who is in reality bathing in the 'Madman Jacuzzi' that is the decorative water fountain at the roundabout . . . at Tom Redcam Avenue . . . their spirits gone and leave them . . . mad djinn take them over . . . how they going to be whole again . . . how we going to be whole again?

She went home and prepared for the cycle of mourning. The lay-down-in-your-room-for-days-and-nights-on-end . . . the can't-eat-so-you-lose-thirteen-pounds-in-two-weeks, so your skin becomes grey and ashen, so every stinking depressing song that they can find in the record library at RJR and JBC, they play it when you turn on the radio . . . all those songs, a whole world of songs of 'Ooooh he is gone and I'm so blue . . . and if he don't come back to me I will surely die' . . . the waking up at five o'clock with the memory and the pain on you, the afraid to go out in public because everybody knows you got another beating . . . the hoping he will call and give you a good explanation . . . hoping he will just call. She went home to lie down in her darkened room and to prepare for another death. But this time something else happened. First she did not turn on the radio . . . she found an old hymn book and did something she had seen her mother do years ago when she was a child . . . she started to sing from this old worn book . . . songs of her childhood when she was unspoiled and innocent and thought there was but one man in the world for her and that she and him were going to go and live happily ever after. She sang, 'All Things Bright and Beautiful,' she sang, 'I am Weak but Thou Art Mighty, Hold Me with Thy Powerful Hand' . . . 'Bread of Heaven Feed Me Till I Want No More'. Then when the five o'clock awakening hour of memories came . . . she woke up . . . but instead of lying down and letting the memories cover her . . . she got up, dressed and went to sit on her verandah and she stared into the dark just-before-dawn sky, until the light separated itself from the darkness right before her eyes . . . just left out the darkness and came to the front of the sky . . . maybe that's not what really happened but that is how it looked . . . and further, it looked like the darkness of the just-before-dawn, just left . . . one minute it was dark, the next minute the pink and white and silver and baby-blue dawn was just roseate in the sky . . . and she put on her walking shoes and went out on the road. Early morning is a good time to talk to the creator, early morning and late at night. At those times, most people still sleeping and the lines of communication are not crowded . . . so she walk, so she talk . . . so she asking what she do to deserve all this . . . especially this new shame? . . . and she got an answer, quick, quick. The answer said . . . who do you love? And in what order do you love? You love all the everybodys before you love who created love (thank the one who created love for creating love). And you love all the everybodys . . . like they were the ones who create love and you don't love yourself as the temple of the one who created love . . . what you're doing is doing it all the wrong way around. You can't love right till you have it in the proper order . . . and so she got her answer . . .

And so every morning when the five o'clock hour of the memories came, she got up and saluted the dawn and she began to watch for the light and as soon as she saw the light separate itself from the night . . . she stared with all her might into the light . . . that way she was drawing much of the light into herself. She began to hear some natural directions coming to her . . . sometimes from the mouth of the most unlikely people. A taxi man, a lady in the market, a little boy who just wrote in his funny little cockroach writing one day . . . this little boy just wrote on a piece a paper 'HE is in you' . . . and he gave it to her . . . and if the creator is in you . . . you can't be meditating on 'if I don't have you I'm surely gonna die' . . . no, now you're going to *live*! With all this she begin to clear a space in her thinking, a place of possibility . . . a place of . . . 'I don't have to live like that . . . I can live like this . . . a place of making a choice, you can stay near to the way of dying for romantic love or you can find a new way to live . . . live so that your eyes reflect all the light you have drawn into you and you don't envy anybody anything because all you need is inside you, and if you don't feel so good one day, that is all right too . . . because once you know that place you will always want to be doing what is necessary to get back to it.' So it is from this clearing of possibility that she was beaming when she walked into a room and saw him. A room full of people and she sees him and all she can do is to laugh out loud . . . and then he started laughing and they are now both laughing and recognizing each other and moving towards each other in recognition and greeting. 'You have come,' he says. She says, 'Oh yes.'

At some point in her searchings, someone had told her it was possible to obtain anything you desired by visualizing it and concentrating upon it, that way you could make it real . . . something in her had always refused really to believe in this as a thing to do for herself . . . and now she understood why . . . now that she saw him she understood why, her imagination was limited, she could not possibly envisage anyone as wonderful as this . . . how much better are the things the creator has for us than what we would want for ourselves . . . he says this just as she was thinking the same thing.

Now they are sitting on the floor drinking the same cup of tea and smoking the same cigarette . . . because they are not angels . . . they drink too many cups of tea and smoke too many cigarettes . . . while they talk and talk and talk, and sometimes they just get really quiet and just become like quietness itself. They are both the same height, they are both the same colouring and they both have hair that is inclined to turbulence . . . there is one great difference. His hands are very big . . . so big that sometimes she can hide her hands in his. Because they are not angels, sometimes his stomach hurts, and she makes him comfort root tea then. They are only together for a short time. One day he said . . . 'You must go into the town without me and see how we bear separation.' So she went . . . she went and stood in a crowd listening to a man speaking of the power of the kissing flower and her stomach began to hurt. And she turned around and saw him standing behind her. So they were never separated again till the morning they had to part for a lifetime. He took her in the early morning . . . at the five o'clock hour of the memories, to a pasture . . . and there waiting was a mighty horse with mighty wings . . . and he placed her astride the horse and he embraced her and said, 'We have much to do in this lifetime.' And then he said, 'Always' and she said, 'Absolutely' and the horse rose into the sky with her seated in the safe place between its wings. She looked not to the left or right or behind her and the horse followed a swift wind, taking her home. When it reached over her house it circled low like an airplane, stretched its legs stiff like an airplane, then bent its knees to cushion the landing . . . and touched ground. She slid from its back . . . thanked it for the ride and offered it sugar and water and a rest . . . it said, 'No thanks but an uneven number of red roses would do, they being sweet and moist enough,' and that it needed no rest, as it had to return to its master. Now she walks into rooms, and they say how strange, she is one person yet she never looks alone . . . and if they think it and ask it of her, she says, 'No, I'm not alone for I have met myself and I never will be alone again.'

Angelita and Golden Days

Angelita began to notice that everytime Golden Days pass through the market, something happen. Hear him coming now singing 'Golden Days'. Like Mario Lanza, 'Golden Days' he was singing and Golden Days they call him because his skin was such an unusual golden colour . . . when the sun shone on him he seemed to glow and his hair was kind of rusty looking and he was always dressed in something gold, like today he was wearing a gold-coloured shirt with a big gold star on one pocket and he was singing rich and golden, like Mario Lanza. Sometimes he did not pass through the market for weeks, then one Saturday morning (you would hear him before you saw him) his notes would float above the heads of the Saturday morning market crowd, rising high above the calls of . . . 'Yam and potato, ah me have it . . . buy something from me nuh nice lady . . . camphor balls and seasoning . . . pattanize me nuh darling,' . . . the wailing keening of the sankeys sung by the revivalists and the dub dance-hall tapes barking from scattered tape decks and the bad words and the laughter and the greetings and scandal that was the soundtrack accompanying Saturday morning in the market. Miraculously, Golden Days' voice could rise above all that, hear him now coming, singing 'Golden Days' . . . and finally when he would reach up to where Angelita was sitting selling her callaloo and pak choi. Half-Indian Angelita with her dress lapped between her thighs, sitting quietly before her buckets of greens. Angelita just sit there, she never bother to call out to anybody to come and buy from her, her beauty just draw them and they would just come and buy her fresh greens that she and her father grow.

A lot of men want Angelita . . . but she did not want them. She didn't seem to want anybody, she just come into the market, sell her greens and then pick up her bucket and the little low bench she sat on and leave, like she came, by herself.

Now Golden Days came up to her and says what he always says, 'How much for the dollar bundle of callaloo?' And Angelita smiles and says, 'One dollar fifty.'

Golden Days bend down in one smooth movement like you fold a hinged object and he is looking into her eyes now, 'How much you say for the one dollar bundle of callaloo?' Angelita blushes and smiles, 'I say one dollar fifty.'

Soon after Golden Days left the market a big commotion broke out. Two police jeeps filled with Harmon Barracks men draw up outside the market. Then the police and soldier rush over to the fish section and started to turn over the fish carts and at that moment the market turned into a sea for Angelita. Honestly, it's like she found herself under the ocean and all the people in the market began to look like fish fluttering up and down. The women in bright dresses and head ties and aprons looked like parrot fish and butter fish and the men could be doctor fish and the fat fish man could be a grouper and Angelita hurrying towards the market gate with small quick steps was, of course, an angelfish.

The next day she found out that the police uncovered two sub-machine guns in Pappa Tappa's cart well wrapped in newspaper and plastic. Pappa Tappa said he had no idea how they had reached into his cart, and the police said he should come with them to Harmon Barracks and see if he could remember.

Something always happen when Golden Days pass through. When Angelita thought about it, she wondered if Golden Days was a science man.

One morning she woke up and made tea for her father. She realized that he was late getting up. Usually he was up just before the sun . . . so she take the tea and brought it to him in bed. He took it from her and said, 'I don't feel so good.' So she said maybe he should take some cerassee tea instead of the green tea she had made him, and he said no, he would drink the green tea.

Angelita's father was quite old but most mornings he was up, watering the callaloo and pak choi and feeding the chickens. But that day he stayed inside all day lying in his single bed covered up under a thin blanket, just singing feebly to himself. So Angelita feed the chickens and water the greens and worked in the yard all that day. She killed a chicken and made soup for her father, but he barely drank a little. Next day it was the same thing. Angelita told her father to come and make her take him to the doctor. He said no, but drank some cerassee tea that evening. That night, in the middle of the night, she woke up for her father was snoring so loudly. She got up to turn him over. Before she could do it, it seemed somebody turned him over and the snoring cut off sharp and Angelita screamed out into the night. You one leave now Angelita.

After the funeral, Angelita never knew what to do except to go on living like she always lived when her father was alive. She was his only child and her mother had died when she was small. The little one-roomed house they had shared was on a little piece of captured land. Everybody who lived there was a squatter. They all moved closer to Angelita for a while after the funeral, but somehow she preferred to be on her own. The men tried to get her more than ever, so she had to sleep with her bed up against the door and to read Psalm 4 every night . . . also she believed that her father's spirit was looking after her. One night before she fell asleep it occurred to her that she had not seen Golden Days for some time.

And the next day she saw him. She hear him first, across the market, his singing seemed to be coming directly at her. It's like he was surrounding her with his singing and her head felt light and she felt light, her whole body was like it was lifted up by his singing. Then the crowd before her just parted and Golden Days was standing before her. He came up to her and he was still singing and the sound of his singing making her feel lighter and lighter, then he bent down in the one smooth movement . . . like you fold something with well-oiled hinges, and still singing, and said to her (he dropped his voice soft, soft), he said, 'Angel, I hear you father gone and you have nobody now? Is true, Angel?' And Angelita started to cry, right there in the market. It's the most she cried since her father's death. Angelita was accustomed to keeping her feelings to herself. Where she came from you either feel bad or you feel good. Those were the only feelings Angelita knew about . . . she never discussed any other feelings . . . funny thing about Angelita, she relied very much on the pictures in her mind to tell her what to do. Like when she wanted to know if something was right for her to do, she would wait and see if a picture of a lavender flower came into her mind. If she thought to do something and the lavender flower came into her mind, then she would know it was all right to do it.

She thought in pictures a lot, there was so much inside her that she saw, she sometimes wondered if she was 'quiet mad' like how she had seen the market turn into a sea when the policemen came and turned over the cart. Angelita kept these things to herself in case people thought she was really mad. She didn't talk a lot because the world in her head was so much prettier than what was around her. Like she always saw herself with a really special man like a movie star, nobody in her surroundings was good enough. She knew that Indian women were supposed to be very passionate, well, she had never been overcome by passion for any of the men around her. Angelita had a vision of herself, living in a nice big pink and white house with a man who looked like a movie star; none of the men she knew looked like that.

'Baby girl, cry, you will feel better,' said Golden Days. But Angelita did not feel better, she just wanted to do more than cry, she wanted to let out some of all that was inside her, to share her secret world with somebody else.

'Leave your load a little and come make me and you go for a walk,' says Golden Days. He turned to the woman sitting across from Angelita, 'Watch her bundle for her no Miss B . . . she don't feel so good,' and before Angelita could think of saying anything, the lavender flower just opened up inside her head. She go with Golden Days, out through the market and she walk and talk and cry and she never went back to the market that day.

She find out that Golden Days was a dreamer too and that freed her to tell him all about the things that go on inside her. Golden Days understood.

His dreams had to do with music. One day he was going to be a big singer, big time ballad singer. He wanted to sing mainly love songs, he did not want to sing any dance hall music and slackness. And Angelita told him how she wanted to live in a pink and white house and grow flowers, not callaloo and pak choi and that she hated the smell of chickens. The only thing Golden Days wondered about was how were they going to manage because he wanted a gold house . . . then she thought some more and said, maybe a pink and gold house? And she laughed.

Everybody wondered what a pretty girl like Angelita was doing with Golden Days. She pick and pick . . . beauty and the beast, ugly cockroach cut pretty silk. But every hoe have them stick a bush and Golden Days was Angelita's. Golden Days' dreams of becoming a great ballad singer were not going well. He had a beautiful voice, like when he sang 'You never walk alone' or 'I believe' at any stage show, the crowd would go wild. But as far as records was concerned the crowd just wanted slackness. Some singers make some big money off singing some of the nastiest, dirtiest songs anybody could ever think off . . . songs that make a man shame to think him have a mother . . . but the public was buying that right now.

Golden Days say him heart and conscience could never give him to sing any song like that. Angelita hated the slack music too. She saw their match as the first step towards living a clean and pretty life . . . no, no slackness for Golden Days and Angelita. But things were getting harder and harder. At first there was a magic quality to life with Golden Days. He had moved into the little room with her, but first he fixed it up. He painted the walls with some cheap white paint and then he bought a child's paint box. He painted Angelita's hands and feet with different colours and made her press them all over the walls. She made a patchwork quilt by going down to a garment factory and getting a bunch of 'scrapses' cheap and the little room was just cosy and glowing with colour and love. It was not a pink and gold house, it was more like a jewelled cave.

But plenty days if Angelita did not sell some greens, no pot would bubble on the fire. Angelita began to wonder what Golden Days really did every day when he left the yard to go to the studio with his exercise book of songs. He began to lose weight. Sometimes he picked up a little painting job here and there. Almost a year went by and Angelita began to wonder if he was really ever going to make it. Then one day a producer saw Golden Days outside the studio gate, he remembered him from seeing him on a Christmas morning stage show . . . he said he had just the song for a voice like his, it was called 'Slackness goes cultural' and it was a nasty degrading set of lyrics done to the tune of 'When you walk through a storm'. Golden Days shook his head . . . the producer took out his wallet, Golden Days remembered Angelita and how sad she looked as she was still cleaning out the chicken coop, how the corners of her pretty mouth turned down, as they were no nearer to realizing the dream of the pink and gold house and he said to the producer, 'Let me see it.'

That night when he went home he was very quiet, and just before he fell asleep he said to Angelita, 'I cut a tune today you know' . . . and she said (as if she knew), 'What kind a tune?' and he didn't answer her for a long time. Then across the darkness in the little room came Golden Days' beautiful rich voice, the voice that had such power over Angelita . . . this time the voice was low and thin . . . instead of making her feel excited, brushed by fingers of gentle lightning, it made her feel sick and anxious. He said, 'The song slack, well slack too . . . but the money is for you,' and Angelita never answered. She turn her back to him and close her eyes tight tight, because she knew they were losing something she did not want to lose.

From that time, Angelita started to see Golden Days in a different way. He began to look very ordinary, pathetic sometimes, and it was funny, because the song became a great dance-hall hit and Golden Days became very popular, but Angelita become more and more repulsed by him. The room they shared did not look like a magic cave anymore, it looked like pickney foolishness and she really didn't feel proud when other people asked her if it was her boy friend who sang 'Slackness goes cultural' . . . . . . Angelita wanted a clean life. Golden Days realized that she had turned away from him, but suddenly there were a lot of other women, pretty uptown girls who were cheeking him after he did stage shows, women who loved to hear the slackness, and when Angelita finally told him that he was not to come back to the room because she couldn't stand him . . . because he had killed her dreams and that she couldn't bear it now when he put his hands on her . . . that is how Golden Days became the slackest singer in Jamaica.

Shilling

She knew they had begun to call her Shilling. One afternoon as she was making her way past the group of boys congregated outside the Cross Roads Post Office, one of the boys took a shilling from his pocket, came up to her and said, 'I hear that you cost one shilling.'

Shilling was a slim, fair-skinned girl and we all knew that she was 'bad' . . . that she slept with boys, that she went to night clubs, that is why she was always falling asleep in class. Last term, Shilling had dyed her hair jet black, bleached it blonde, dyed it red, very red, light brown, dark brown. Every week she had changed the colour of her hair, till the headmistress had spoken in assembly about girls who made themselves look cheap and ridiculous by dying their hair every colour of the rainbow, who, if they could not comport themselves in a reasonable manner should seek educational opportunities elsewhere. That was one thing about our headmistress, she never said simple words when she could say complex words . . . in fact we had to translate for some of the non English-loving girls, that she meant if Shilling did not stop dyeing her hair, she would be expelled. Actually, Shilling was given the name not because of what the vicious schoolgirls and -boys said about her selling herself for a shilling, it was because she had dyed her hair an extraordinary shade of platinum blonde which had turned kind of green, and Helen, the school wit, had said that her hair had the appearance of a gangrenous shilling . . .

It seems she wanted to change herself so badly . . . up until last term she had been a quiet, dreamy, not-so-bright girl, then in one term she became the notorious Shilling.

Shilling knows no one will believe her, that up until last term she was as innocent as the most innocent girl in the school . . . certainly more innocent than a lot of them. That all she ever wanted was to get through fifth form, get a job, maybe in a bank, meet a nice man, marry and have babies. That was the extent of her ambition. There were teachers predicting that some girls were going to be great scientists like Marie Curie and others were going to be great leaders of society; all Shilling ever wanted was to get married and have some babies. She used to draw her wedding-dress in class all the time and cancel her name with the name of whichever boy she had a crush on at the time. She designed elaborate gowns trimmed with lace which she drew as loops around the hem, around the sleeves, travelling up and down the bodice of these dream wedding-dresses. She always drew herself with a long veil covering her face, because she was going to be a virgin when she got married. She would also draw her 'change' dress, or going-away dress, the dress in which she would go off to her honeymoon . . . that's all she ever wanted . . . and in good order.

Then she fell in love with him. She saw him at a Manning cup match. He was dark and not too tall and he had the most wonderful face, big eyes with bags under them and a nose with a slight hump in the middle like a boxer. He moved very lightly when he walked, which was unusual for a football player, he moved more like a dancer. She took one look at him sitting there in the grandstand with his arm around his girlfriend's chair and she fell in love, absolutely and fatally, the way only a sixteen-year-old girl could fall in love. Somehow, it did not seem to matter to her that he was sitting with his arm around his girlfriend's chair. Her eyes registered the girl but she did not care, all she saw was him. The girl was very stuck-up-looking, boasy and conceited, she thought. She had good skin and a pretty enough face, but she looked heavy, like she was of the earth, you couldn't imagine her dreaming about flying as Shilling so often dreamt, that she grew wings and was flying to see her mother in New York. She was a very confident girl though, confident of her relationship with him. And anybody but

Shillling could see that he thought the sun and moon resided in this girl and rose and set only when she gave them permission. When the peanut man came around with his song that always made schoolboys and girls laugh . . . 'Mi say just done bake and them sweeter than a cake, a so them criss mi say a no teet miss' . . . . everyone laugh except his girlfriend. She just told him to get her some peanuts and he jumped over three rows of seats to get them. When he came back, he sat down and shelled the peanuts for her; she held out her palm and received them as her due. Shilling never watched the match, she just watched him shelling peanuts for this girl and the girl accepting them by sticking her palm out sideways and never even saying thank you, just looking at the match and eating the peanuts when her palm was full enough. Shilling thought to herself, what an awful girl, what does he see in her, if it were her, she would have been shelling the peanuts for him. When the match was over, he took his blazer from the empty seat next to him and draped it across her shoulders like a queenly cape. She just accepted it as her due, sort of shrugged her shoulders into it, and then they walked hand in hand from the grandstand through the tunnel out of the stadium.

She had to find out who he was. So she asked a boy she knew who went to his school, and he told her his name. She asked about the girlfriend and the guy told her the girlfriend was wealthy, she drove her own car and that everyone thought she was very stuck up and boasy. He (her love) came from a poor but decent family and the girlfriend had him 'soft': everybody knew that.

The next week, she saw him at a bus stop; he was standing with some other boys, one of whom she knew. She made sure she passed close to him, making sure that he saw her; she felt so thrilled just to be near him, just to walk across his shadow. When she saw the boy she knew, she asked for an introduction to him. Of course the boy told him, because the next time she saw him and his girlfriend, the girl looked at her and laughed out loud, then whispered something to him and he just grinned. But she didn't care, she was absolutely in love with him. She cancelled his name with hers, she tried to divine his presence into her life by a schoolgirl's mystic and romantic mathematics . . . add up all the numbers on your bus ticket then match the final number to this rhyme: One for sorrow, two for joy, three for girl, four for boy, five for silver, six for gold, seven for a secret that's never been told. She always seemed to be getting seven, not four for boy as she hoped.

Her wedding-dresses became more elaborate and now she drew him beside her as the groom. She tried to draw his boxer's nose and his deep eyes. And she began to imagine every detail of the ceremony. How she would walk up the aisle to Patti La Belle and the Blue Belles singing 'Down the Aisle'; how she would promise to love and honour and yes, obey him; how they would drive away in a car marked 'Just Married'; and how he would crush his lips passionately to hers . . . just like in a Mills and Boon story. She was so absorbed in this dream that she began to get into bad trouble at school for day-dreaming and inattention. Once, the geography teacher came up behind her as she was drawing a particularly ornate wedding-dress. The woman snatched the drawing out of her hand and ridiculed her before the class, told her that in order to get married she would need a groom and that men were not fond of useless women; that she was useless, good for nothing but day-dreaming . . . the class roared with glee. Encouraged by her success the teacher went on, 'Imagine if your husband wanted you to cook him a good meal, you would day-dream while everything on the stove burnt to nothing' . . . she ended this humiliating lesson by giving her two hundred lines to write after school, 'I am not a bride and the classroom is not a chapel. I must work hard and study Geography while I am in Geography class.' Two hundred lines. When she got home it was quite late and she missed seeing him at the bus stop.

She began to go to every Manning cup match in which he played, to go to every school function where she might see him. She was boarding with a family as her mother was in New York working, so she told them lies to explain why she came in late every evening. She had Science club, and Bible Knowledge group and games after school and rehearsals for plays which never took place. She did not care, all she wanted was to see him.

Then Donna A. had her sweet-sixteenth birthday party. She was not a close friend, but she was invited to the party. The truth is, Donna wanted to get as many presents as possible; the girls had a competition to see who could have the most elaborate sweet-sixteen party, who could get the most presents. One girl had received six of the same sets of *Desert Flower* hand lotion and cologne sets, four sets of *Blue Grass* cologne and at least ten handkerchief sets, two shorty pyjamas and fourteen boxes of Cadbury chocolate from one party. Shilling was very happy to attend because Donna told her that he would be there, with his girl friend yes, but he would be there.

Her mother sent her from New York a blue satin dress. The skirt was shaped like a bell and there was a large artificial rose to one side of the skirt. It was a beautiful dress, she thought she looked lovely, very grown-up. Then when she saw him arrive with the girl she felt like a child. He was dressed like all the other boys in a dark suit, white shirt and tie, but his girlfriend was in a scarlet chiffon dress, close-fitting and low cut. They looked like the perfect couple; when they entered the room everybody turned to look at them. They danced only with each other. Both sides of the Drifters' LP. Up on the roof, you only dance with somebody to two sides of a Drifters' LP if you had practically pledged your life to them; you would rent a tile into happiness. Eventually, some sweating boy asked her to dance and she manoeuvered him close to where they were dancing together tight as two five cents in a ten cent. No breeze could blow between them . . . eyes closed, moving as one body. You could tell they were used to dancing with each other . . . 'This magic moment while your lips are close to mine will last forever, forever till the end of time.'

Shilling closed her eyes, moved closer to the sweating boy, and transported herself across the dance floor into his arms. It was really she he was dancing with not Miss High-and-Mighty in the red chiffon dress. Then she boxed him. Right there on the dance floor. One minute they were the perfect couple, then, who knows what she said to him or him to her and what the reply was, but she slapped him just like some woman in a movie and walked off the dance floor leaving him standing there looking like a fool. Everybody stopped dancing and began asking what was the matter and he was just looking stunned and holding his face, and she was just pushing her way out across the verandah, down through the yard, jangling the keys to her car. Then he ran after her. Everybody discussed what happened for a while then they settled down again to enjoy the party. Shilling kept telling everyone how she thought the girl was dreadful. Most people said yes, but he was just totally in love with her so he would put up with anything. About an hour later he came back to the party without her. When everybody started to ask him what was the matter, he refused to answer. He just went over to the bar where he stood for a long while drinking beer after beer and not saying anything . . . she just sat and watched him. Then he walked over to her and held out his hand; he didn't say a word, he was so sure of her response. Shilling just went to him, he pulled her close and they danced for a long while. He never said anything, she felt sweat (or tears) running down his cheek and he kept his eyes shut tight.

Shilling never used to dance really close with anybody, but now she was pasted right up against him. She was so happy, she was trembling. It was a good thing they hardly moved or she would never have followed his steps. She was shaking with joy, she was in his arms!

Later in the night he spoke. He said, 'Come with me,' and she followed him round to the back of the house where there was an empty room. It looked like an abandoned maid's quarters, a single bed with an old beat-up mattress and a little broken locker. He took her there, laid her down on the mattress and with great force and no tenderness emptied his humiliation into her. He never even called her darling or asked how she was, nothing . . . but she was glad to be there for him, now he would probably realize which girl really loved him. She opened her eyes which were screwed tight with the pain and shock and happiness and hope and that is when she saw the other boys standing in the room.

Bella Makes Life

He was embarrassed when he saw her coming toward him. He wished he could have just disappeared into the crowd and kept going as far away from Norman Manley Airport as was possible. Bella returning. Bella come back from New York after a whole year. Bella dressed in some clothes which make her look like a checker cab. What in God's name was a big forty-odd-year-old woman who was fat when she leave Jamaica, and get worse fat since she go to America, what was this woman doing dressed like this? Bella was wearing a stretch-to-fit black pants, over that she had on a big yellow and black checked blouse, on her feet was a pair of yellow booties, in her hand was a big yellow handbag and she had on a pair of yellow-framed glasses. See ya Jesus! Bella no done yet, she had dyed her hair with red oxide and Jherri curls it till it shine like it grease and spray. Oh Bella what happen to you? Joseph never ever bother take in her anklet and her big bracelets and her gold chain with a pendant, big as a name plate on a lawyer's office, marked 'Material Girl'.

Joseph could sense the change in Bella through her letters. When she just went to New York, she used to write him DV every week.

Dear Joe Joe,

How keeping my darling? I hope fine. I miss you and the children so till I think I want to die. Down in Brooklyn here where I'm living, I see a lot of

Jamaicans, but I don't mix up with them. The lady who sponsor me say that a lot of the Jamaicans up here is doing wrongs and I don't want to mix up with those things as you can imagine. You know that I am only here to work some dollars to help you and me to make life when I come home. Please don't have any other woman while I'm gone. I know that a man is different from a woman, but please do try and keep yourself to yourself till we meet and I'm saving all my love for you.

Your sweet, sweet,

Bella

That was one of the first letter that Bella write Joseph, here one of the last letters.

Dear Joseph,

What you saying? I really sorry that my letter take so long to reach you and that the Post Office seem to be robbing people money left, right and centre. Man, Jamaica is something else again. I don't write as often as I used to because I working two jobs. My night job is doing waitressing in a night club on Nostrand Avenue, the work is hard but tips is good. I make friends with a girl on the job named Yvonne and sometimes she and I go with some other friends on a picnic or so up to Bear Mountain. I guess that's where Peaches says she saw me. I figure I might as well enjoy myself while I not so old yet.

Your baby,

Bella

Enjoy herself? This time Joseph was working so hard to send the two children to school clean and neat, Joseph become mother and father for them, even learn to plait the little girl hair. Enjoy himself? Joseph friend them start to laugh after him because is like him done with woman.

Joseph really try to keep himself to himself. Although the nice, nice woman who live at the corner of the next road. Nice woman you know, always talking so pleasant to him. Joseph make sure that the two of them just remain social friends . . . and Bella up in New York about she gone a Bear Mountain, make blabbamouth Peaches come back from New York and tell everybody in the yard how she buck up Bella a picnic and how Bella really into the Yankee life fully.

It was Norman, Joseph's brother, who said that Bella looked like a checker cab. Norman had driven Joseph and the children to the airport in his van to meet Bella, because she write to say she was coming with a lot of things. When the children saw her they jumped up and down yelling mama come, mama come . . . When Norman saw her (he was famous for his wit), he said, 'Blerd Naught, a Bella dat, whatta way she favour a checker cab.' When Bella finally cleared her many and huge bags from Customs and come outside, Joseph was very quiet, he didn't know quite how to greet the new Bella. Mark you Bella was always 'nuff' but she really was never as wild as this. She ran up to Joseph and put her arms around him. Part of him felt a great sense of relief that she was home, that Joseph and Bella and their two children were a family once more.

Bella was talking a little too loudly, 'Man, I tell you those customs people really give me a warm time, oh it's so great to be home though, it was so cold in New York!' As she said this she handed her winter coat with its mock fur collar to her daughter who staggered under the weight of it. Norman, who was still chuckling to himself over his checker cab joke, said, 'Bwoy, Bella a you broader than Broadway'. Bella said, 'Tell me about it' . . .

They all went home. Joseph kind of kept quiet all the way home and allowed the children to be united with their mother . . . she was still Mama Bella though, asking them about school, if they had received certain parcels she had sent and raising an alarm how she had sent a pair of the latest high-top sneakers for the boy and that they had obviously stolen them at the Post Office.

Every now and again she leaned across and kissed Joseph. He was a little embarrassed but pleased. One time she whispered in his ear, 'I hope you remember I've been saving all my love for you.' This was a new Bella though, the boldness and the forwardness was not the old Bella who used to save all her love for when they were alone together with the bolt on the door.

She would not encourage too much display of affection before the children. That change in Bella pleased Joseph. There were some other changes in Bella that did not please him so much though. Like he thought that all the things in the many suitcases were for their family. No sir! While Bella brought quite a few things for them, she had also brought a lot of things to sell and many evenings when Joe Joe come home from work just wanting a little peace and quiet, to eat his dinner, watch a little TV and go to him bed and hug up his woman, his woman (Bella) was out selling clothes and 'things'. She would go to different offices and apartment buildings and she was always talking about which big important brown girl owed her money . . . Joseph never loved that. He liked the idea of having extra money, they now had a number of things they could not afford before, but he missed the old Bella who he could just sit down and reason with and talk about certain little things that a one have store up in a one heart . . . Bella said, America teach her that if you want it, you have to go for it. Joe Joe nearly ask her if she want what? The truth is that Joe Joe felt that they were doing quite all right. He owned a taxi which usually did quite well, they lived in a Government Scheme which gave you the shell of a house on a little piece of land under a scheme called 'Start to build up your own home' . . . and they had built up quite a comfortable little two-bedroom house with a nice living-room, kitchen, bathroom and verandah. What did Bella mean when she said, 'You have to make it?' As far as Joe Joe was concerned, he had made it. And him was not going to go and kill himself to get to live upon Beverley Hills because anyhow the people up there see all him taxi friend them drive up that way to visit him, them would call police and set guard dog on them . . . Joe Joe was fairly contented . . . is what happen to Bella?

'Come ya little Bella, siddown, make me ask you something. You no think say that you could just park the buying and selling little make me and you reason bout somethings?'

'Joe Joe, you live well yah. I have three girls from the bank coming to fit some dresses and if them buy them then is good breads that.'

After a while, Joe Joe stopped trying to reclaim their friendship. After a month, Bella said she wanted to go back to New York. Joe Joe asked her if she was serious.

'You know that nobody can't love you like me, Joe Joe.'

Joe Joe wondered about that. Sometimes he looked at the lady at the corner of the next road, their social friendship had been severely curtailed since Bella returned home, but sometimes he found himself missing the little talks they used to have about life and things in general.

She was a very simple woman. He liked her style, she was not fussy. Sometimes he noticed a man coming to her, the man drive a Lada, look like him could work with the Government, but him look married too. You know how some man just look married? Well this man here look like a man who wear a plaid bermuda shorts with slippers when him relax on a Sunday evening, and that is a married man uniform.

When Joe Joe begun to think of life without Bella, the lady at the corner of the next road began to look better and better to him.

'So Bella really gone back a New York?'

'Yes mi dear, she say she got to make it while she can.'

'Make what?'

'It!'

'A wha it so?'

'You know . . . Oh forget it.'

And that is what Joe Joe decided to do. The lady, whose name was Miss Blossom, started to send over dinner for Joe Joe not long after Bella went back to New York.

'Be careful of them stew peas and rice you a eat from that lady they you know, mine she want tie you.' Joe Joe said, 'True?' and continued eating the dinner that Miss Blossom had sent over for him. He didn't care what Peaches said, her mouth was too big anyway. He just wanted to enjoy eating the 'woman food'. Somehow, food taste different, taste more nourishing when a woman cook it.

Bella write to say that she was doing fine.

Dear Joe Joe,

I know you're mad with me because you didn't want me to come back to the States, but darling, I'm just trying to make it so that you and me and the children can live a better life and stop having to box feeding outta hog mouth.

Now that really hurt Joe Joe. He would never describe their life together as that . . . True, sometimes things had been tight but they always had enough to eat and wear. Box feeding outta hog mouth . . . that was the lowest level of human existence and all these years he thought they were doing fine, that is how Bella saw their life together . . . well sir. Joe Joe was so vex that him never even bother to reply to that letter.

Joe Joe started to take Miss Blossom to pictures and little by little the line of demarcation between social friends and sweetheart just blurred. Joe Joe tell her that the married man better stop come to her and Miss Blossom say him was only a social friend and Joe Joe say 'Yes', just like how him and her was social friend . . . and she told him he was too jealous and him say yes he was, 'But I don't want to see the man in here again,' and she said, 'Lord, Joe Joe.'

Little by little Miss Blossom started to look after the children and look after Joe Joe clothes and meals, is like they choose to forget Bella altogether. Then one Christmas time Bella phone over the grocery shop and tell Mr Lee to tell Joe Joe that she was coming home for Christmas.

Well to tell the truth, Joe Joe never want to hear anything like that. Although Miss Blossom couldn't compare to Bella because Bella was the first woman Joe Joe ever really love . . . Joe Joe was feeling quite contented and he was a simple man, him never really want to take on Bella and her excitement and her 'got to make it'. Anyway, him tell Miss Blossom say Bella coming home and she say to him, 'Well Joe, I think you should tell her that anything stay too long will serve two masters, or two mistresses as the case might be.'

Joe Joe say, 'Mmmmm . . . but remember say Bella is mi baby mother you know and no matter what is the situation, respect is due.'

Miss Blossom said that, 'When Bella take up herself and gone to New York and leave him, she should know that respect was due to him too.' Joe Joe say, 'Yes,' but him is a man who believe that all things must be done decently and in good order, so if him was going to put away Bella him would have to do it in the right and proper way. Miss Blossom say she hope that when Bella gone again him don't bother ask her ti nuttin. Joe Joe became very depressed.

If Bella looked like a checker cab the first time, she looked like Miami Vice this time, inna a pants suit that look like it have in every colour flowers in the world and the colour them loud! And Bella broader than ever . . . Oh man. Norman said, 'Bees mus take up Bella inna that clothes dey. Any how she pass Hope Gardens them must water her.'

Bella seemed to be oblivious to the fact that Joe Joe was under great strain. She greeted him as if they had parted yesterday, 'Joe Joe what you saying sweet pea.' Joe Joe just looked at her and shook his head and said, 'Wha happen Bella?' They went home but Joe Joe felt like he and the children went to meet a stranger at the airport. Bella had become even stranger than before to Joe Joe. He began to wonder exactly what she was doing in America, if she really was just waitressing at that club. Bella told him that he should come forward, because this was the age of women's liberation, and Joe Joe told her that maybe she should liberate her backside outta him life because he couldn't take her.

Bella cried and said how much she loved him. Then things became really intense and it was like a movie and they had to turn up the radio really high to prevent the children from hearing them.

Joe Joe decided to just bite him tongue while Bella was home. He took to coming home very late all through the Christmas season because the house was usually full of Bella's posse including the 'Yvonne' of Bear Mountain Fame, and when they came to visit the house was just full up of loud laughing and talking and all kinds of references that Joe Joe didn't understand. The truth was that he was really dying for Bella to leave. He really didn't much like the woman she had become. First of all everything she gave to him or the children, she tell them how much it cost . . . 'Devon, beg you don't bother to take that Walkman outside, is Twenty-Nine Ninety-Nine, I pay for it at Crazy Eddies,' or, 'Ann-Marie, just take time with that jagging suit, I pay Twenty-Three Dollars for it in May's Department Store. Oh Lord.'

Bella also came armed with two junior Jherri curls kits and one day Joe Joe come home and find him son and him daughter heads well Jherri curls off.

Joe Joe nearly went mad. 'So you want Devon fi tun pimp or what?'

'Joe, you really so behind time, you should see all the kids on my block.'

'On your block, well me ago black up you eye if you don't find some way fi take that nastiness outta my youth man hair, him look like a cocaine seller. Bella what the hell do you, you make America turn you inna idiat? Why you don't just gwan up there and stay then, me tired a you foolishness . . .'

Bella couldn't believe that Joe Joe was saying this to her . . . then she told him that he was a worthless good-for-nuttin and that him never have no ambition, him just want to stay right inna the little two by four (their house) and no want no better and that she was really looking for a better way and that he clearly did not fit into her plans.

Joe Joe say him glad she talk what was in her mind because now him realize say that she was really just a use him fi convenience through nobody a New York no want her. Bella said . . . then he said . . . Oh, they said some things to each other!

One thing though, Bella catch her fraid and try wash out the Jherri curls outta Devon hair. No amount of washing could bring it round. The barber had was to nearly bald the little boy head and he spent the worse Christmas of his life.

All his friends 'smashed' him as they passed by. As New Year done so, Bella pack up herself and went back to New York.

Joe Joe make a two weeks pass before him make a check by Miss Blossom. The whole Christmas gone him never see her. He figured that she had gone to spend the holidays in the country with her family. When he asked in the yard where she was, they told him they had no idea where she was gone, and that her room was empty. Joe Joe felt like a beaten man. He went home and decided to just look after him two children and just rest within himself. About a month later he was driving home when he saw somebody looking like Miss Blossom standing at the corner of the road. It look like Miss Blossom, but no, it couldn't be, this woman was dressed like a punk . . . in full black, she had on a black socks with a lace frothing over the top of her black leather ankle boots. A big woman. He slowed the cab down and said, 'Blossom . . . where you was?' . . . and then he thought quickly, 'No, don't bother answer me . . . you go to New York, right?'

'No,' said Blossom, 'I was in Fort Lawdadale. You seem to think only Bella one can go to America.'

Joe Joe never even bother ask her if she want a drive, him just draw a gear and move off down the road, then him go inside him house and slam the door.

Before him drop asleep, it come to him that maybe what him should do was to find an American woman who wanted to live a simple life in Jamaica. Him know a rasta man who have a nice yankee woman like that . . .

Summer Lightning and other stories

Olive Senior

Olive Senior is one of Jamaica's most exciting creative talents. *Summer Lightning* is her first collection of short stories.

Her setting is rural Jamaica; her heroes are the naive and the vulnerable, who bring to life with power and realism issues such as snobbery, ambition, jealousy, faith and love.

Written in vivid, colourful detail, these rich, compelling stories recreate with sensitivity and wit a whole range of emotions, from childhood hope to brooding melancholy. Each is told with an affectionate and poignant perception of you and I at our best and worst.

ISBN 0 582 78627 4

From the reviews of *Summer Lightning:*

'This is the most exciting collection of short stories to come out of the Caribbean for a very long time and it places Olive Senior in the front rank of short-fiction writers.'

Anna Rutherford in KUNAPIPI

'Senior's achievement is to address ominous issues uniquely, by cataloguing, with wit and affection, the lilting speech and loping gait of the local population.'

TIMES LITERARY SUPPLEMENT

Arrival of the Snake-Woman and other stories

Olive Senior

Olive Senior, winner of the first Commonwealth Writers Prize in 1987 with *Summer Lightning*, has produced another magical volume of stories, many of which are written from a child's perspective of an alien adult world in the villages and towns of Jamaica. Senior moves with ease between past and present, and catches the haunted discontent of the older characters who take more prominence in her writing now.

As always in her work there is the acerbic humour, the musicality of the Jamaican creole, and more and more, a sense of wistfulness and wisdom.

ISBN 0 582 03170 2

Foreday Morning

Sam Selvon

'The sea of life which moves to and fro always fascinates me,' wrote Selvon in 1949. Here are stories and articles from one of the Caribbean's best-known writers. They present sharp, vivid portraits of Trinidadian life and reflect Selvon's love of the island he left behind for London, and eventually Canada. Even after years abroad, Selvon's writing is charged with passion for the Caribbean and its immense beauty as though it is a bond he cannot break.

ISBN 0 582 03982 7

Voiceprint

An Anthology of Oral and Related Poetry from the Caribbean.

Selected and edited by Stewart Brown, Mervyn Morris and Gordon Rohlehr.

This exciting anthology breaks new ground in its coverage of poetic voices from the English-speaking Caribbean. It brings together for the first time a wealth of different styles, musical expressions, rhythms and dialects in the form of poems, songs, elegies, laments, dub, parang, hosay, calypsos and many more to show the richness and range of the oral tradition in West Indian poetry.

ISBN 0 582 78629 0